PUT NOT YOUR FAITH IN (MERCHANT) PRINCES . . .

T'heonax turned it over and over. "What a weapon!"

" . . .Where are other three blasters?" van Rijn asked.

"What other three?" T'heonax stared at him.

"We have six . . .I give-um all to good sir Delp, here."

"What?"

Delp leaned at the human, cursing. . . .

"He's plotting mutiny!"

Wace threw Sandra to the deck and himself above her. The air grew dense with missiles.

Van Rijn turned ponderously to grab the sailor in charge of Tolk. But that Drak'ho had already sprung away to Delp's defense.

"Now, go bring in an army to fetch us out of here. Quick, before someone notices."

The Herald nodded, threshed his wings and was gone into the sky. . . .

"All saints in Heaven!" choked Wace. "You touched off a civil war just to get your messenger away?"

"You perhaps know a better method?" asked van Rijn.

"The shock at the end, after the action, when you suddenly realize that you've been cheering the wrong side, or the weaklings aren't, or some-basic law has been ignored . . .the color, smell, taste of an alien world, a nonhuman society, a globular cluster or the universe seen from the very edge of lightspeed . . .these things Poul shows better than anyone."

—Larry Niven

Books by
POUL ANDERSON

THE LONG WAY HOME
THE MAN WHO COUNTS
THE NIGHT FACE
THE PEREGRINE
QUESTION AND ANSWER
WORLD WITHOUT STARS
THE WORLDS OF POUL ANDERSON

The Saga of Dominic Flandry:
ENSIGN FLANDRY
FLANDRY OF TERRA

From Ace Science Fiction

SF

THE
MAN WHO COUNTS

by
POUL ANDERSON

SF
ace books
A Division of Charter Communications Inc.
A GROSSET & DUNLAP COMPANY
360 Park Avenue South
New York, New York 10010

THE MAN WHO COUNTS

originally published as *War of the Wingmen*

An ACE Book

Second Ace Edition: February 1978
Third Ace Edition: July 1979

Cover art by Michael Whelan

4 6 8 0 9 7 5 3
Manufactured in the United States of America

Introduction

THE MAN WHO COUNTS

Thinking about this early novel after a lapse of years,
I believe I can see what its wellsprings are. They
include the old pulp conventions of storytelling and a
desire to change or, at any rate, spoof these: Falstaff,
Long John Silver, and other amiable literary rogues, as
well as a few real figures from the Renaissance: L.
Sprague de Camp's unique combination of humor and
adventure: above all, Hal Clement's marvelously de-
tailed and believable fictional worlds. I do not say that
The Man Who Counts matches any of its inspirers.
Certainly I would write it a bit differently today. Yet it
does represent my first serious venture into planet-
building and the first full-scale appearance of Nicholas
van Rijn. Thus I remain fond of it.

After being serialized in *Astounding* (today's

Analog) it had a paperback edition. The latter was badly copy-edited and saddled with the ludicrous title *War of the Wing-Men*. I am happy that now, at last, the proper text and name can be restored.

Planet-building is one of the joyous arts, if you have that sort of mind. The object is to construct a strange world which is at the same time wholly consistent, not only with itself but with what science knows of such matters. Any extra-scientific assumptions you make for story purposes—e.g., faster-than-light travel—should not be necessary to the world itself. So, taking a star of a given mass, you calculate how luminous it must be, how long the year is of a planet in a given orbit around it, how much irradiation that planet gets, and several more things. (Of course. I simplify here, since you ought also to take account of the star's age, its chemical composition, etc.) These results will be basically influential on surface features of the planet, kind of life it bears, evolution of that life, and so on endlessly. There is no rigid determinism: at any given stage, many different possibilities open up. However, those which you choose will in their turn become significant parameters at the next stage . . . until at last, perhaps, you get down to the odor of a flower and what it means to an alien individual.

Because science will never know everything, you are allowed reasonable guesses where calculation breaks down. Nonetheless—quite apart from flaws which sharp-eyed readers may discover in your facts or logic—you can be pretty sure that eventually science *will* make discoveries which cast doubt, to say the very least, on various of your assumptions. History will have moved on, too, in directions you had not foreseen for your imaginary future. You are invited to play what Clement calls "the game" with this unrevised text of mine.

I was saved from making one grievous error, by my wife. Looking over my proposed life cycle of the Diomedeans, she exclaimed, "Hey, wait, you have the females flying thousands of miles each year while they're the equivalent of seven months pregnant. It can't be done. I know." I deferred to the voice of experience and redesigned. As I have remarked elsewhere, planet-building ought to be good therapy for the kind of mental patient who believes he's God.

Despite the hazards, I've come back to it again and again, always hoping that readers will share some of the pleasure therein.

Poul Anderson

I

Grand Admiral Syranaxhyr Urnan, hereditary Commander-in-Chief of the Fleet of Drak'ho, Fisher of the Western Seas, Leader in Sacrifice, and Oracle of the Lodestar, spread his wings and brought them together again in an astonished thunderclap. For a moment, it snowed papers from his desk.

"No!" he said. "Impossible! There's some mistake."

"As my Admiral wills it," Chief Executive Officer Delp hyr Orikan bowed sarcastically. "The scouts saw nothing."

Anger crossed the face of Captain T'heonax hyr Urnan, son of the Grand Admiral and therefore heir apparent. His upper lip rose until the canine tushes showed, a white flash against the dark muzzle.

"We have no time to waste on your insolence, Executive Delp," he said coldly. "I would advise my father to dispense with an officer who has no more respect."

Under the embroidered cross-belts of office Delp's big frame tautened. Captain T'heonax glided one step toward him. Tails curled back and wings spread, instinctive readiness for battle, until the room was full of their bodies and their hate. With a calculation which made it seem accidental, T'heonax dropped a hand to the obsidian rake at his waist. Delp's yellow eyes blazed and his fingers clamped on his own tomahawk.

Admiral Syranax's tail struck the floor. It was like a fire-bomb going off. The two young nobles jerked, remembered where they were, and slowly, muscle by muscle laying itself back to rest under the sleek brown fur, they relaxed.

"Enough!" snapped Syranax. "Delp, your tongue will flap you into trouble yet. T'heonax I've grown bored with your spite. You'll have your chance to deal with personal enemies, when I am fish food. Meanwhile, spare me my few able officers!"

It was a firmer speech than anyone had heard from him for a long time. His son and his subordinate recalled that this grizzled, dim-eyed, rheumatic creature had once been the conqueror of the Maion Navy—a thousand wings of enemy leaders had rattled grisly from the mastheads—and was still their chief in the war against the Flock. They assumed the all-fours crouch of respect and waited for him to continue.

"Don't take me so literally, Delp," said the admiral

in a milder tone. He reached to the rack above his desk and got down a long-stemmed pipe and began stuffing it with flakes of dried sea driss from the pouch at his waist. Meanwhile, his stiff old body fitted itself more comfortable into the wood-and-leather seat. "I was quite surprised, of course, but I assume that our scouts still know how to use a telescope. Describe to me again exactly what happened."

"A patrol was on routine reconnaisance about 30 obdisai north-north-west of here," said Delp with care. "That would be in the general area of the island called . . . I can't pronounce that heathenish local name, sir; it means Banners Flew."

"Yes, yes," nodded Syranax. "I have looked at a map now and then, you know."

T'heonax grinned. Delp was no courtier. That was Delp's trouble. His grandfather had been a mere Sailmaker, his father never advanced beyond the captaincy of a single raft. That was after the family had been ennobled for heroic service at the Battle of Xarit'ha, of course—but they had still been very minor peers, a tarry-handed lot barely one cut above their own crewfolk.

Syranax, the Fleet's embodied response to these grim days of hunger and uprooting, had chosen officers on a basis of demonstrated ability, and nothing else. Thus it was that simple Delp hyr Orikan had been catapulated in a few years to the second highest post in Drak'ho. Which had not taken the rough edges off his education, or taught him how to deal with *real* nobles.

If Delp was popular with the common sailors, he was

all the more disliked by many aristocrats—a parvenu, a boor, with the nerve to wed a sa Axollon! Once the old admiral's protecting wings were folded in death—

T'heonax savored in advance what would happen to Delp hyr Orikan. It would be easy enough to find some nominal charge.

The executive gulped. "Sorry, sir," he mumbled. "I didn't mean . . . we're still so new to this whole sea . . . well. The scouts saw this drifting object. It was like nothing ever heard of before. A pair of 'em flew back to report and ask for advice. I went to look for myself. Sir, it's true!"

"A floating object—six times as long as our longest canoe—like ice, and yet not like ice—" The admiral shook his gray-furred head. Slowly, he put dry tinder in the bottom of his firemaker. But it was with needless violence that he drove the piston down into the little hardwood cylinder. Removing the rod again, he tilted fire out into the bowl of his pipe, and drew deeply.

"The most highly polished rock crystal might look a bit like that stuff, sir," offered Delp. "But not so bright. Not with such a *shimmer*."

"And there are animals scurrying about on it?"

"Three of them, sir. About our size, or a little bigger, but wingless and tailless. Yet not just animals either . . . I think . . . they seem to wear clothes and —I don't think the shining thing was ever intended as a boat, though. It rides abominably, and appears to be settling."

"If it's not a boat, and not a log washed off some beach," said T'heonax "then where, pray tell, is it from? The Deeps?"

"Hardly, captain," said Delp irritably. "If that were so, the creatures on it would be fish or sea mammals or—well, adapted for swimming, anyway. They're not. They look like typical flightless land forms, except for having only four limbs."

"So they fell from the sky, I presume?" sneered T'heonax.

"I wouldn't be at all surprised," said Delp in a very low voice. "There isn't any other direction left."

T'heonax sat up on his haunches, mouth falling open. But his father only nodded.

"Very good," murmured Syranax. "I'm pleased to see a little imagination around here."

"But where did they fly *from?*" exploded T'heonax.

"Perhaps our enemies of Lannach would have some account of it" said the admiral. "They cover a great deal more of the world every year than we do in many generations; they meet a hundred other barbarian flocks down in the tropics, and exchange news."

"And females," said T'heonax. He spoke in that mixture of primly disapproving voice and lickerish overtones with which the entire Fleet regarded the habits of the migrators.

"Never mind that," snapped Delp.

T'heonax bristled. "You deckswabber's whelp, do you dare—"

"Shut up!" roared Syranax.

After a pause, he went on: "I'll have inquiries made among our prisoners. Meanwhile we had better send a fast canoe to pick up these beings before that object they're on founders."

"They may be dangerous," warned T'heonax.

"Exactly," said his father. "If so, they're better in our hands than if, say, the Lannach'honai should find them and make an alliance. Delp, take the *Nemnis*, with a reliable crew, and crowd sail on her. And bring along that fellow we captured from Lannach, what's his name, the professional linguist—"

"Tolk?" The executive stumbled over the unfamiliar pronunciation.

"Yes. Maybe he can talk to them. Send scouts back to report to me, but stand well off the main Fleet until you're sure that the creatures are harmless to us. Also till I've allayed whatever superstitious fears about sea demons there are in the lower classes. Be polite if you can, get rough if you must. We can always apologize later . . . or toss the bodies overboard. Now, jump!"

Delp jumped.

II

Desolation walled him in.

Even from this low, on the rolling, pitching hull of the murdered skycruiser, Eric Wace could see an immensity of horizon. He thought that the sheer size of that ring, where frost-pale heaven met the gray which was cloud and storm-scud and great marching waves, was enough to terrify a man. The likelihood of death had been faced before, on Earth, by many of his forebears; but Earth's horizon was not so remote.

Never mind that he was a hundred-odd light-years from his own sun. Such distances were too big to be understood: they became mere numbers, and did not frighten one who reckoned the pseudo-speed of a secondary-drive spaceship in parsecs per week.

Even the ten thousand kilometers of open ocean to

this world's lone human settlement, the trading post, was only another number. Later, if he lived, Wace would spend an agonized time wondering how to get a message across that emptiness, but at present he was too occupied with keeping alive.

But the breadth of the planet was something he could see. It had not struck him before, in his eighteen-month stay; but then he had been insulated, psychologically as well as physically, by an unconquerable machine technology. Now he stood alone on a sinking vessel, and it was twice as far to look across chill waves to the world's rim as it had been on Earth.

The skycruiser rolled under a savage impact. Wace lost his footing and slipped across curved metal plates. Frantic, he clawed for the light cable which lashed cases of food to the navigation turret. If he went over the side, his boots and clothes would pull him under like a stone. He caught it in time and strained to a halt. The disappointed wave slapped his face, a wet salt hand.

Shaking with cold, Wace finished tucking the last box into place and crawled back toward the entry hatch. It was a miserable little emergency door, but the glazed promenade deck, on which his passengers had strolled while the cruiser's gravbeams bore her through the sky, was awash, its ornate bronze portal submerged.

Water had filled the smashed engine compartment when they ditched. Since then it had been seeping around twisted bulkheads and strained hull plates, until the whole thing was about ready for a last long dive to the sea bottom.

Wind passed gaunt fingers through his drenched hair and tried to hold open the hatch when he wanted to close it after him. He had a struggle against the gale . . . Gale? Hell, no! It had only the velocity of a stiffish breeze—but with six times the atmospheric pressure of Earth behind it, that breeze struck like a Terrestrial storm. Damn PLC 2987165 II! Damn the PL itself, and damn Nicholas van Rijn, and most particularly damn Eric Wace for being fool enough to work for the Company!

Briefly, while he fought the hatch, Wace looked out over the coaming as if to find rescue. He glimpsed only a reddish sun, and great cloud-banks dirty with storm in the north, and a few specks which were probably natives.

Satan fry those natives on a slow griddle, that they did not come to help! Or at least go decently away while the humans drowned, instead of hanging up there in the sky to gloat!

"Is all in order?"

Wace closed the hatch, dogged it fast, and came down the ladder. At its foot, he had to brace himself against the heavy rolling. He could still hear waves beat on the hull, and the wind-yowl.

"Yes, my lady," he said. "As much as it'll ever be."

"Which isn't much, not?" Lady Sandra Tamarin played her flashlight over him. Behind it, she was only another shadow in the darkness of the dead vessel. "But you look a saturated rat, my friend. Come, we have at least fresh clothes for you."

Wace nodded and shrugged out of his wet jacket and kicked off the squelching boots. He would have frozen up there without them—it couldn't be over five degrees C.—but they seemed to have blotted up half the ocean. His teeth clapped in his head as he followed her down the corridor.

He was a tall young man of North American stock, ruddy-haired, blue-eyed, with bluntly squared-off features above a well-muscled body. He had begun as a warehouse apprentice at the age of twelve, back on Earth, and now he was the Solar Spice & Liquors Company's factor for the entire planet known as Diomedes. It wasn't exactly a meteoric rise—Van Rijn's policy was to promote according to results, which meant that a quick mind, a quick gun, and an eye firmly held to the main chance were favored. But it had been a good solid career, with a future of posts on less isolated and unpleasant worlds, ultimately an executive position back Home and—and what was the use, if alien waters were to eat him in a few hours more?

At the end of the hall, where the navigation turret poked up, there was again the angry copper sunlight, low in the wan smoky-clouded sky, south of west as day declined. Lady Sandra snapped off her torch and pointed to a coverall laid out on the desk. Beside it were the outer garments, quilted, hooded, and gloved, he would need before venturing out again into the pre-equinoctial springtime. "Put on everything," she said. "Once the boat starts going down, we will have to leave in a most horrible hurry."

"Where's Freeman van Rijn?" asked Wace.

"Making some last-minute work on the raft. That

one is a handy man with the tools, not? But then, he was once a common spacehand.''

Wace shrugged and waited for her to leave.

''Change, I told you,'' she said.

''But—''

''Oh.'' A thin smile crossed her face. ''I thought not there was a nudity taboo on Earth.''

''Well . . . not exactly, I guess, my lady . . . but after all, you're a noble born, and I'm only a trader—''

''From republican planets like Earth come the worst snobs of all,'' she said. ''Here we are all human beings. Quickly, now, change. I shall turn my back if you desire.''

Wace scrambled into the outfit as fast as possible. Her mirth was an unexpected comfort to him. He considered what luck always appeared to befall that pot-bellied old goat Van Rijn.

It wasn't right!

The colonists of Hermes had been, mostly, a big fair stock, and their descendants had bred true: especially the aristocrats, after Hermes set up as an autonomous grand duchy during the Breakup. Lady Sandra Tamarin was nearly as tall as he, and shapeless winter clothing did not entirely hide the lithe full femaleness of her. She had a face too strong to be pretty—wide forehead, wide mouth, snub nose, high cheekbones—but the large smoky-lashed green eyes, under heavy dark brows, were the most beautiful Wace had ever seen. Her hair was long, straight, ash-blond, pulled into a knot at the moment but he had seen it floating free under a coronet by candlelight—

''Are you quite through, Freeman Wace?''

"Oh . . . I'm sorry, my lady. I got to thinking. Just a moment!" He pulled on the padded tunic, but left it unzipped. There was still some human warmth lingering in the hull. "Yes. I beg your pardon."

"It is nothing." She turned about. In the little space available, their forms brushed together. Her gaze went out to the sky. "Those natives, are they up there yet?"

"I imagine so, my lady. Too high for me to be sure, but they can go up several kilometers with no trouble at all."

"I have wondered, Trader, but got no chance to ask. I thought not there could be a flying animal the size of a man, and yet these Diomedeans have a six-meter span of bat wings. How?"

"At a time like *this* you ask?"

She smiled. "We only wait now for Freeman van Rijn. What else shall we do but talk of curious things?"

"We . . . help him . . . finish that raft soon or we'll all go under!"

"He told me he has just batteries enough for one cutting torch, so anyone else is only in the way. Please continue talking. The high-born of Hermes have their customs and taboos, also for the correct way to die. What else is man, if not a set of customs and taboos?" Her husky voice was light, she smiled a little, but he wondered how much of it was an act.

He wanted to say: We're down in the ocean of a planet whose life is poison to us. There is an island a few score kilometers hence, but we only know its direction vaguely. We may or may not complete a raft in time, patched together out of old fuel drums, and we may or may not get our human-type rations loaded on it in time, and it may or may not weather the storm brewing there in the north. Those were natives who swooped low above us a few hours ago, but since then they have ignored us . . . or watched us . . . anything except offer help.

Someone hates you or old Van Rijn, he wanted to say. Not me, I'm not important enough to hate. But Van Rijn is the Solar Spice & Liquors Company, which is a great power in the Polesotechnic League, which is *the* great power in the known galaxy. And you are the Lady Sandra Tamarin, heiress to the throne of an entire planet, if you live; and you have turned down many offers of marriage from its decaying, inbred aristocracy, publicly preferring to look elsewhere for a father for your children, that the next Grand Duke of Hermes may be a man and not a giggling clothes horse; so no few courtiers must dread your accession.

Oh, yes, he wanted to say, there are plenty of people who would gain if either Nicholas van Rijn or Sandra Tamarin failed to come back. It was a calculated gallantry for him to offer you a lift in his private ship, from Antares where you met, back to Earth, with stopovers at interesting points along the way. At the very least, he can look for trade concessions in the Duchy. At best . . . no, hardly a formal alliance; there's too much hell in him; even you—most strong and fair and innocent —would never let him plant himself on the High Seat of your fathers.

But I wander from the subject, my dear, he wanted to say; and the subject is, that someone in the spaceship's crew was bribed. The scheme was well-hatched; the someone watched his chance. It came when you landed on Diomedes, to see what a really new raw planet is like, a planet where even the main continental outlines have scarcely been mapped, in the mere five years that a spoonful of men have been here. The chance came when I was told to ferry you and my evil old boss to those sheer mountains, halfway around this world, which have been noted as spectacular scenery. A bomb in the main generator . . . a slain crew, engineers and stewards gone in the blast, my co-pilot's skull broken when we ditched in the sea, the radio shattered . . .and the last wreckage is going to sink long before they begin to worry at Thursday Landing and come in search of us and assuming we survive, is there the slightest notice-able chance that a few skyboats, cruising a nearly unmapped world twice the size of Earth, will happen to see three human flyspecks on it?

Therefore, he wanted to say, since all our schemings and posturings have brought us merely to this, it would be well to forget them in what small time remains, and kiss me instead.

But his throat clogged up on him, and he said none of it.

"So?" A note of impatience entered her voice. "You are very silent, Freeman Wace."

"I'm sorry, my lady," he mumbled. "I'm afraid I'm no good at making conversation under . . . uh, these circumstances."

"I regret I have not qualifications to offer to you the consolations of religion," she said with a hurtful scorn.

A long gray-bearded comber went over the deck

outside and climbed the turret. They felt steel and plastic tremble under the blow. For a moment, as water sheeted, they stood in a blind roaring dark.

Then, as it cleared, and Wace saw how much farther down the wreck had burrowed, and wondered if they would even be able to get Van Rijn's raft out through the submerged cargo hatch, there was a whiteness that snatched at his eye.

First he didn't believe it, and then he wouldn't believe because he dared not, and then he could no longer deny it.

"Lady Sandra." He spoke with immense care; he *must* not scream his news at her like any low-born Terrestrial.

"Yes?" She did not look away from her smoldering contemplation of the northern horizon, empty of all but clouds and lightning.

"There, my lady. Roughly south-east, I'd guess sails, beating up-wind."

"What?" It was a shriek from her. Somehow, that made Wace laugh aloud.

"A boat of some kind," he pointed. "Coming this way."

"I didn't know the natives were sailors," she said, very softly.

"They aren't, my lady—around Thursday Landing," he replied. "But this is a big planet. Roughly four times the surface area of Earth, and we only know a small part of one continent."

"Then you know not what they are like, these sailors?"

"My lady, I have no idea."

III

Nicholas van Rijn came puffing up the companionway at their shout. "Death and damnation!" he roared. "A boat, do you say, *ja?* Better for you it is a shark, if you are mistaken. By damn!" He stumped into the turret and glared out through saltencrusted plastic. The light was dimming as the sun went lower and the approaching storm clouds swept across its ruddy face. "So! Where is it, this pestilential boat?"

"There, sir," said Wace. "That schooner—"

"Schooner! Schnork! Powder and balls, you cement head, that is a yawl rig . . .no, wait, by damn, there is a furled square sail on the mainmast too, and, yes, an outrigger— *Ja,* the way she handles, she must have a regular rudder— Good saints help us! A bloody-be-damned-to-blazes dugout!"

"What else do you expect, on a planet without met-

als?'' said Wace. His nerves were worn too thin for him
to remember the deference due a merchant prince.

"Hm-m-m . . . coracles, maybe so, or rafts or
catamarans— Quick, dry clothes! Too cold it is for
brass monkeys!''

Wace grew aware that Van Rijn was standing in a
puddle, and that bitter sea water streamed from his
waist and legs. The storeroom where he had been at
work must have been awash for—for hours!

"I know where they are, Nicholas." Sandra loped
off down the corridor. It slanted more ominously every
minute, as the sea pushed in through a ruined stern.

Wace helped his chief off with the sopping coverall.
Naked, Van Rijn suggested . . . what was that extinct
ape? . . . a gorilla, two meters tall, hairy and huge-
bellied, with shoulders like a brick warehouse, loudly
bawling his indignation at the cold and the damp and
the slowness of assistants. But rings flashed on the
thick fingers and bracelets on the wrists, and a little St.
Dismas medal swung from his neck. Unlike Wace, who
found a crew cut and a clean shave more practical Van
Rijn let his oily black locks hang curled and perfumed
in the latest mode, flaunted a goatee on his triple chin
and intimidating waxed mustaches beneath the great
hook nose.

He rummaged in the navigator's cabinet, wheezing,
till he found a bottle of rum. "Ahhh! I knew I had the
devil-begotten thing stowed somewhere." He put it to
his frogmouth and tossed off several shots at a gulp.
"Good! Fine! Now maybe we can begin to be like
self-respectful humans once more, *nie?*''

He turned about, majestic and globular as a planet, when Sandra came back. The only clothes she could find to fit him were his own, a peacock outfit of lace-trimmed shirt, embroidered waistcoat, shimmersilk culottes and stockings, gilt shoes, plumed hat, and holstered blaster. "Thank you," he said curtly. "Now, Wace, while I dress, in the lounge you will find a box of Perfectos and one small bottle applejack. Please to fetch them, then we go outside and meet our hosts."

"Holy St. Peter!" cried Wace. "The lounge is under water!"

"Ah?" Van Rijn sighed, woebegone. "Then you need only get the applejack. Quick, now!" He snapped his fingers.

Wace said hastily: "No time, sir. I still have to round up the last of our ammunition. Those natives could be hostile."

"If they have heard of us, possible so," agreed Van Rijn. He began donning his natural-silk underwear. *"Brrr!* Five thousand candles I would give to be back in my office in Jakarta!"

"To what saint do you make the offer?" asked Lady Sandra.

"St. Nicholas, natural—my namesake, patron of wanderers and—"

"St. Nicholas had best get it in writing," she said.

Van Rijn purpled; but one does not talk back to the heiress apparent of a nation with important trade concessions to offer. He took it out by screaming abuse after the departing Wace.

It was some time before they were outside; Van Rijn

got stuck in the emergency hatch and required pushing, while his anguished basso obscenities drowned the nearing thunder. Diomedes' period of rotation was only twelve and a half hours, and this latitude, thirty degrees north, was still on the winter side of equinox; so the sun was toppling seaward with dreadful speed. They clung to the lashings and let the wind claw them and the waves burst over them. There was nothing else they could do.

"It is no place for a poor old fat man," snuffed Van Rijn. The gale ripped the words from him and flung them tattered over the rising seas. His shoulder-length curls flapped like forlorn pennons. "Better I should have stayed at home in Java where it is warm, not lost my last few pitiful years out here."

Wace strained his eyes into the gloom. The dugout had come near. Even a landlubber like himself could appreciate the skill of its crew, and Van Rijn was loud in his praises. "I nominate him for the Sunda Yacht Club, by damn, yes, and enter him in the next regatta and make bets!"

It was a big craft, more than thirty meters long, with an elaborate stempost, but dwarfed by the reckless spread of its blue-dyed sails. Out-rigger or no, Wace expected it to capsize any moment. Of course, a flying species had less to worry about if that should happen than—

"The Diomedeans." Sandra's tone was quiet in his ear, under shrill wind and booming waters. "You have dealt with them for a year and a half, not? What can we await for from them?"

Wace shrugged. "What could we expect from any random tribe of humans, back in the Stone Age? They might be poets, or cannibals, or both. All I know is the Tyrlanian Flock, who are migratory hunters. They always stick by the letter of their law—not quite so scrupulous about its spirit, of course, but on the whole a decent tribe."

"You speak their language?"

"As well as my human palate and Techno-Terrestrial culture permit me to, my lady. I don't pretend to understand all their concepts, but we get along—" The broken hull lurched. He heard some abused wall rend, and the inward pouring of still more sea, and felt the sluggishness grow beneath his feet. Sandra stumbled against him. He saw that the spray was freezing in her brows.

"That does not mean I'll understand the local language" he finished. "We're farther from Tyrlan than Europe from China."

The canoe was almost on them now. None too soon: the wreck was due to dive any minute. It came about, the sails rattled down, a sea anchor was thrown and brawny arms dug paddles into the water. Swiftly, then, a Diomedean flapped over with a rope. Two others hovered close, obviously as guards. The first one landed and stared at the humans.

Tyrlan being farther north, its inhabitants had not yet returned from the tropics and this was the first Diomedean Sandra had encountered. She was too wet, cold, and weary to enjoy the unhuman grace of his movements, but she looked very close. She might have to dwell with this race a long time, if they did not murder her.

He was the size of a smallish man, plus a thick meter-long tail ending in a fleshy rudder and the tremendous chiropteral wings folded along his back. His arms were set below the wings, near the middle of a sleek otterlike body, and looked startlingly human, down to the muscular five-fingered hands. The legs were less familiar, bending backward from four-taloned feet which might almost have belonged to some bird of prey. The head, at the end of a neck that would have been twice too long on a human, was round, with a high forehead, yellow eyes with nictitating membranes under heavy brow ridges a blunt-muzzled black-nosed face with short cat-whiskers, a big mouth and the bear-like teeth of a flesheater turned omnivore. There were no external ears, but a crest of muscle on the head helped control flight. Short, soft brown fur covered him; he was plainly a male mammal.

He wore two belts looped around his "shoulders," a third about his waist, and a pair of bulging leather pouches. An obsidian knife, a slender flint-headed ax, and a set of bolas were hung in plain view. Through the thickening dusk, it was hard to make out what his wheeling comrades bore for weapons—something long and thin, but surely not a rifle, on this planet without copper or iron . . .

Wace leaned forward and forced his tongue around the grunting syllables of Tyrlanian: "We are friends. Do you understand me?"

A string of totally foreign words snapped at him. He

shrugged, ruefully, and spread his hands. The Diomedean moved across the hull—bipedal, body slanted forward to balance wings and tail—and found the stud to which the humans' lashings were anchored. Quickly, he knotted his own rope to the same place.

"A square knot," said Van Rijn, almost quietly. "It makes me homesick."

At the other end of the line, they began to haul the canoe closer. The Diomedean turned to Wace and pointed at his vessel. Wace nodded, realized that the gesture was probably meaningless here, and took a precarious step in that direction. The Diomedean caught another rope flung to him. He pointed at it, and at the humans, and made gestures.

"I understand," said Van Rijn. "Nearer than this they dare not come. Too easy their boat gets smashed against us. We get this cord tied around our bodies, and they haul us across. Good St. Christopher, what a thing to do to a poor creaky-boned old man!"

"There's our food, though," said Wace.

The skycruiser jerked and settled deeper. The Diomedean jittered nervously.

"No, no!" shouted Van Rijn. He seemed under the impression that if he only bellowed loudly enough, he could penetrate the linguistic barrier. His arms windmilled. "*Nie!* Never! Do you not understand, you oatmeal brains? Better to guggle down in your pest-begotten ocean than try eating your food. We die! Bellyache! Suicide!" He pointed at his mouth, slapped his abdomen, and waved at the rations.

Wace reflected grimly that evolution was too flexible. Here you had a planet with oxygen, nitrogen, hydrogen, carbon, sulfur . . . a protein biochemistry forming genes, chromosomes, cells, tissues . . . protoplasm by any reasonable definition . . . and the human who tried to eat a fruit or steak from Diomedes would be dead ten minutes later of about fifty lethal allergic reactions. These just weren't the *right* proteins. In fact, only immunization shots prevented men from getting chronic hay fever, asthma, and hives, merely from the air they breathed of the water they drank.

He had spent many cold hours today piling the cruiser's food supplies out here, for transference to the raft. This luxury atmospheric vessel had been carried in Van Rijn's spaceship, ready-stocked for extended picnic orgies when the mood struck him. There was enough rye bread, sweet butter, Edam cheese, lox, smoked turkey, dill pickles, fruit preserves, chocolate, plum pudding, beer, wine, and God knew what else, to keep three people going for a few months.

The Diomedean spread his wings, flapping them to maintain his footing. In the wan stormy light, the thumbs-turned-claws on their leading edge seemed to whicker past Van Rijn's beaky face like a mowing machine operated by some modernistic Death. The merchant waited stolidly, now and then aiming a finger at the stacked cases. Finally the Diomedean got the idea, or simply gave in. There was scant time left. He whistled across to the canoe. A swarm of his fellows came over, undid the lashings and began transporting boxes. Wace helped Sandra fasten the rope about her. "I'm afraid it will be a wet haul, my lady," he tried to smile.

She sneezed. "So this is the brave pioneering between the stars! I will have a word or two for my court poets when I get home . . . if I do.''

When she was across, and the rope had been flown back, Van Rijn waved Wace ahead. He himself was arguing with the Diomedean chief. How it was done without a word of real language between them, Wace did not know, but they had reached the stage of screaming indignation at each other. Just as Wace set his teeth and went overboard, Van Rijn sat mutinously down.

And when the younger man made his drowned-rat arrival on board the canoe, the merchant had evidently won his point. A Diomedean could air-lift about fifty kilos for short distances. Three of them improvised a rope sling and carried Van Rijn over, above the water.

He had not yet reached the canoe when the skycruiser sank.

IV

The dugout held some hundred natives, all armed,
some wearing helmets and breastplates of hard laminated leather. A catapult, just visible through the dark,
was mounted at the bows; the stern held a cabin, made
from sapling trunks chinked with sea weed, that tow-
ered up almost like the rear end of a medieval caravel.
On its roof, two helmsmen strained at the long tiller.

"Plain to see, we have found a navy ship," grunted
Van Rijn. "Not so good, that. With a trader, I can talk.
With some pest-and-pox officer with gold braids on his
brain, him I can only shout." He raised small, close-set
gray eyes to a night heaven where lightning ramped. "I
am a poor old sinner," he shouted, "but this I have not
deserved! Do you hear me?"

After a while the humans were prodded between lithe

devil-bodies, toward the cabin. The dugout had begun to run before the gale, on two reef points and a jib. The roll and pitch, clamor of waves and wind and thunder, had receded into the back of Wace's consciousness. He wanted only to find some place that was dry, take off his clothes and crawl into bed and sleep for a hundred years.

The cabin was small. Three humans and two Diomedeans left barely room to sit down. But it was warm, and a stone lamp hung from the ceiling threw a dim light full of grotesquely moving shadows.

The native who had first met them was present. His volcanic-glass dagger lay unsheathed in one hand, and he held a wary lion-crouch; but half his attention seemed aimed at the other one, who was leaner and older, with flecks of gray in the fur, and who was tied to a corner post by a rawhide leash.

Sandra's eyes narrowed. The blaster which Van Rijn had lent her slid quietly to her lap as she sat down. The Diomedean with the knife flicked his gaze across it, and Van Rijn swore. "You little all-thumbs brain, do you let him see what is a weapon?"

The first autochthone said something to the leashed one. The latter made a reply with a growl in it; then turned to the humans. When he spoke, it did not sound like the same language.

"So! An interpreter!" said Van Rijn. "You speakee Angly, ha? Haw, haw, haw!" He slapped his thigh.

"No, wait. It's worth trying." Wace dropped into Tyrlanian: "Do you understand me? This is the only speech we could possibly have in common."

The captive raised his head-crest and sat up on hands and haunches. What he answered was *almost* familiar. "Speak slowly, if you will," said Wace, and felt sleepiness drain out of him.

Meaning came through, thickly: "You do not use a version (?) of the Carnoi that I have heard before."

"Carnoi—" Wait, yes, one of the Tyrlanians had mentioned a confederation of tribes far to the south, bearing some such name. "I am using the tongue of the folk of Tyrlan."

"I know not that race (?). They do not winter in our grounds. Nor do any Carnoi as a regular (?) thing, but now and then when all are in the tropics (?) one of them happens by, so—" It faded into unintelligibility.

The Diomedean with the knife said something, impatiently, and got a curt answer. The interpreter said to Wace:

"I am Tolk, a *mochra* of the Lannachska—"

"A what of the what?" said Wace.

It is not easy even for two humans to converse, when it must be in different patois of a language foreign to both. The dense accents imposed by human vocal cords and Diomedean ears—they heard farther into the subsonic, but did not go quite so high in pitch, and the curve of maximum response was different—made it a slow and painful process indeed. Wace took an hour to get a few sentences' worth of information.

Tolk was a linguistic specialist of the Great Flock of Lannach; it was his function to learn every language that came to his tribe's attention, which were many. His title might, perhaps, be rendered Herald, for his duties included a good deal of ceremonial announcements and he presided over a corps of messengers. The Flock was at war with the Drak'honai, and Tolk had been captured in a recent skirmish. The other Diomedean present was named Delp, and was a high-ranking officer of the Drak'honai.

Wace postponed saying much about himself, less from a wish to be secretive than from a realization of how appalling a task it would be. He did ask Tolk to warn Delp that the food from the cruiser, while essential to Earthlings, would kill a Diomedean.

"And why should I tell him that?" asked Tolk, with a grin that was quite humanly unpleasant.

"If you don't, said Wace, "it may go hard with you when he learns that you did not."

"True." Tolk spoke to Delp. The officer made a quick response.

"He says you will not be harmed unless you yourselves make it necessary," explained Tolk. "He says you are to learn his language so he can talk with you himself."

"What was it now?" interrupted Van Rijn.

Wace told him. Van Rijn exploded. "What? What does he say? Stay here till—Death and wet liver! I tell that filthy toad—" He half rose to his feet. Delp's wings rattled together. His teeth showed. The door was flung open and a pair of guards looked in. One of them carried a tomahawk, another had a wooden rake set with chips of flint.

Van Rijn clapped a hand to his gun. Delp's voice crackled out. Tolk translated: "He says to be calm."

After more parley, and with considerable effort and guesswork on Wace's part: "He wishes you no harm, but he must think of his own people. You are something new. Perhaps you can help him, or perhaps you are so harmful that he dare not let you go. He must have time to find out. You will remove all your garments and implements, and leave them in his charge. You will be provided other clothing, since it appears you have no fur."

When Wace had interpreted for Van Rijn, the merchant said, surprisingly at ease: "I think we have no choice just now. We can burn down many of them, *ja*. Maybe we can take the whole boat. But we cannot sail it all the way home by ourselves. If nothing else, we would starve en route, *nie?* Were I younger, yes, by good St. George, I would fight on general principles. Single-handed I would take him apart and play a xylophone on his ribs. and try to bluster his whole nation into helping me. But now I am too old and fat and tired. It is hard to be old, my boy—"

He wrinkled his sloping forehead and nodded in a wise fashion. "But, where there are enemies to bid against each other, that is where an honest trader has a chance to make a little bit profit!"

V

"First," said Wace, "you must understand that the world is shaped like a ball."

"Our philosophers have known it for a long time," said Delp complacently. "Even barbarians like the Lannach'honai have an idea of the truth. After all, they cover thousands of obdisai every year, migrating. We're not so mobile, but we had to work out an astronomy before we could navigate very far."

Wace doubted that the Drak'honai could locate themselves with great precision. It was astonishing what their neolithic technology had achieved, not only in stone but in glass and ceramics; they even molded a few synthetic resins. They had telescopes, a sort of astrolabe, and navigational tables based on sun, stars, and the two small moons. However, compass and chronometer require iron, which simply did not exist in any noticeable quantity on Diomedes.

Automatically, he noted a rich potential market. The primitive Tyrlanians were avid for simple tools and weapons of metal, paying exorbitantly in the furs, gems, and pharmaceutically useful juices which made this planet worth the attention of the Polesotechnic League. The Drak'honai could use more sophisticated amenities, from clocks and slide rules to Diesel engines—and were able to meet proportionately higher prices.

He recollected where he was: the raft *Gerunis*, headquarters of the Chief Executive Officer of the Fleet; and that the amiable creature who sat on the upper deck and talked with him was actually his jailer.

How long had it been since the crash—fifteen Diomedean days? That would be more than a week, Terrestrial reckoning. Several per cent of the Earthside food was already eaten.

He had lashed himself into learning the Drak'ho tongue from his fellow-prisoner Tolk. It was fortunate that the League had, of necessity, long ago developed the principles by which instruction could be given in minimal time. When properly focused, a trained mind need only be told something once. Tolk himself used an almost identical system; he might never have seen metal, but the Herald was semantically sophisticated.

"Well, then," said Wace, still haltingly and with gaps in his vocabulary, but adequately for his purposes, "do you know that this world-ball goes around the sun?"

"Quite a few of the philosophers believe that," said Delp. "I'm a practical (?) one myself, and never cared much one way or another."

"The motion of your world is unusual. In fact, in many ways this is a freak place. Your sun is cooler and redder than ours, so your home is colder. This sun has a *mass* . . . what do you say? . . . oh, call it a weight not much less than that of our own; and it is about the same distance. Therefore Diomedes, as we call your world, has a year only somewhat longer than our Earth's. Seven hundred eighty-two Diomedean days, isn't it? Diomedes has more than twice the diameter of Earth, but lacks the heavy materials found in most worlds. Therefore its *gravity*—hell!—therefore I only weigh about one-tenth more here than I would at home."

"I don't understand," said Delp.

"Oh, never mind," said Wace gloomily.

The planetographers were still puzzling about Diomedes. It didn't fall into either of the standard types, the small hard ball like Earth or Mars, or the gas giant with a collapsed core like Jupiter or 61 Cygni C. It was intermediate, with a mass of 4.75 Earths; but its overall density was only half as much. This was due to the nearly total absence of all elements beyond calcium.

There was one sister freak, uninhabitable; the remaining planets were more or less normal giants, the sun a G8 dwarf not very different from other stars of that size and temperature. It was theorized that because of some improbable turbulence, or possibly an odd magnetic effect—a chance-created cosmic mass spectrograph—there had been no heavy elements in the local section of the primordial gas cloud. . . . But why hadn't there at least been a density-increasing molecular collapse at the center of Diomedes? Sheer mass-pressure ought to have produced degeneracy. The most plausible answer to that was, the minerals in the body of this world were not normal ones, being formed in the absence of such elements as chromium, manganese, iron, and nickel. Their crystal structure was apparently more stable than, say, olivine, the most important of the Earth materials condensed by pressure—

The devil with it!

"Never mind that weight stuff," said Delp. "What's so unusual about the motion of Ikt-hanis?" It was his name for this planet, and did not mean "earth" but—in a language where nouns were compared— could be translated "Oceanest," and was feminine.

Wace needed time to reply; the technicalities outran his vocabulary.

It was merely that the axial tilt of Diomedes was almost ninety degrees, so that the poles were virtually in the ecliptic plane. But that fact, coupled with the cool ultra-violet-poor sun, had set the pattern of life.

At either pole, nearly half the year was spent in total night. The endless daylight of the other half did not really compensate; there were polar species, but they were unimpressive hibernators. Even at forty-five degrees latitude, a fourth of the year was darkness, in a winter grimmer than Earth had ever seen. That was as far north or south as any intelligent Diomedeans could live; the annual migration used up too much of their time and energy, and they fell into a stagnant struggle for existence on the paleolithic level.

Here, at thirty degrees north, the Absolute Winter lasted one-sixth of the year—a shade over two Terrestrial months—and it was only (!) a few weeks' flight to the equatorial breeding grounds and back during that time. Therefore the Lannachska were a fairly cultivated people. The Drak'honai were originally from even farther south—

But you could only do so much without metals. Of course, Diomedes had abundant magnesium, beryllium, and aluminum, but what use was that unless you first developed electrolytic technology, which required copper or silver?

Delp cocked his head. "You mean it's always equinox on your Eart'?"

"Well, not quite. But by your standards, very nearly!"

"So that's why you haven't got wings. The Lodestar didn't give you any, because you don't need them."

"Uh . . .perhaps. They'd have been no use to us, anyway. Earth's air is too thin for a creature the size of you or me to fly under its own power."

"What do you mean, thin? Air is . . . is air."

"Oh, never mind. Take my word for it."

How did you explain gravitational potential to a nonhuman whose mathematics was about on Euclid's level? You could say: "Look, if you go sixty-three hundred kilometers upward from the surface of Earth, the attraction has dropped off to one-fourth; but you must go thirteen thousand kilometers upward from Diomedes to diminish its pull on you correspondingly. Therefore Diomedes can hold a great deal more air. The weaker solar radiation helps, to be sure, especially the relatively less ultraviolet. But on the whole, gravitational potential is the secret.

"In fact, so dense is this air that if it held proportionate amounts of oxygen, or even of nitrogen, it would poison me. Luckily, the Diomedean atmosphere is a full seventy-nine per cent neon. Oxygen and nitrogen are lesser constituents: their partial pressures do not amount to very much more than on Earth. Likewise carbon dioxide and water vapor."

But Wace said only: "Let's talk about ourselves. Do you understand that the stars are other suns, like yours, but immensely farther away; and that Earth is a world of such a star?"

"Yes. I've heard the philosophers wonder—I'll believe you."

"Do you realize what our powers are, to cross the space between the stars? Do you know how we can reward you for your help in getting us home, and how our friends can punish you if you keep us here?"

For just a moment, Delp spread his wings, the fur bristled along his back and his eyes became flat yellow chips. He belonged to a proud folk.

Then he slumped. Across all gulfs of race, the human could sense how troubled he was:

"You told me yourself, Eart'ho, that you crossed The Ocean from the west, and in thousands of obdisai you didn't see so much as an island. It bears our own explorings out. We couldn't possibly fly that far, carrying you or just a message to your friends, without some place to stop and rest between times."

Wace nodded, slowly and carefully. "I see. And you couldn't take us back in a fast canoe before our food runs out."

"I'm afraid not. Even with favoring winds all the way, a boat is so much slower than wings. It'd take us half a year or more to sail the distance you speak of."

"But there must be *some* way—"

"Perhaps. But we're fighting a hard war, remember. We can't spare much effort or many workers for your sake.

"I don't think the Admiralty even intends to try."

VI

To the south was Lannach, an island the size of Britain. From it Holmenach, an archipelago, curved northward for some hundreds of kilometers, into regions still wintry. Thus the islands acted as boundary and shield: defining the Sea of Achan, protecting it from the great cold currents of The Ocean.

Here the Drak'honai lay.

Nicholas van Rijn stood on the main deck of the *Gerunis*, glaring eastward to the Fleet's main body. The roughly woven, roughly fitted coat and trousers which a Sailmaker had thrown together for him irritated a skin long used to more expensive fabrics. He was tired of sugar-cured ham and brandied peaches—though when such fare gave out, he would begin starving to death. The thought of being a captured chattel whose wishes nobody need consult was pure anguish. The reflection on how much money the company must be losing for lack of his personal supervision was almost as bad.

"Bah!" he rumbled. "If they would make it a goal of their policy to get us home, it could be done."

Sandra gave him a weary look. "And what shall the Lannachs be doing while the Drak'honai bend all their efforts to return us?" she answered. "It is still a close thing, this war of theirs. Dra'ho could lose it yet."

"Satan's hoof-and-mouth disease!" He waved a hairy fist in the air. "While they squabble about their stupid little territories, the Solar Spice & Liquors is losing a million credits a day!"

"The war happens to be a life-and-death matter for both sides," she said.

"Also for us. *Nie?*" He fumbled after a pipe, remembered that his meerschaums were on the sea bottom, and groaned. "When I find who it was stuck that bomb in my cruiser—" It did not occur to him to offer excuses for getting her into this. But then, perhaps it was she who had indirectly caused the trouble. "Well," he finished on a calmer note, "it is true we must settle matters here, I think. End the war for them so they can do important business like getting me home."

Sandra frowned across the bright sun-blink of waters. "Do you mean help the Drak-honai? I do not care for that so much. They are the aggressors. But then, they saw the wives and little ones hungry—" She sighed. "It is hard to unravel. Let such be so, then."

"Oh, no!" Van Rijn combed his goatee. "We help the other side. The Lannachska."

"What!" She stood back from the rail and dropped her jaw at him. "But . . . but—"

"You see," explained Van Rijn, "I know a little something about politics. It is needful for an honest businessman seeking to make him a little hard-earned profit, else some louse-bound politician comes and taxes it from him for some idiot school or old-age pension. The politics here is not so different from what we do out in the galaxy. It is a culture of powerful aristocrats, this Fleet, but the balance of power lies with the throne—the Admiralty. Now the admiral is old, and his son the crown prince has more to say than is rightful. I waggle my ears at gossip—they forget how much better we hear than they, in this pea-soup-with-sausages atmosphere. I know. He is a hard-cooked one, him that T'heonax.

"So we help the Drak'honai win over the Flock. So what? They are already winning. The Flock is only making guerrilla now, in the wild parts of Lannach. They are still powerful, but the Fleet has the upper hand, and need only maintain *status quo* to win. Anyhow, what can we, who the good God did not offer wings, do at guerrillas? We show T'heonax how to use a blaster, well, how do we show him how to find somebodies to use it on?"

"Hm-m-m . . . yes." She nodded, stiffly. "You mean that we have nothing to offer the Drak'honai, except trade and treaty later on, if they get us home."

"Just so. And what hurry is there for them to meet

the League? They are natural wary of unknowns like us from Earth. They like better to consolidate themselves in their new conquest before taking on powerful strangers, *nie?* I hear the scuttled butt, I tell you; I know the trend of thought about us. Maybe T'heonax lets us starve, or cuts our throats. Maybe he throws our stuff overboard and says later he never heard of us. Or maybe, when a League boat finds him at last, he says *ja*, we pulled some humans from the sea, and we was good to them, but we could not get them home in time.''

''But could they—actually? I mean, Freeman van Rijn, how would *you* get us home, with any kind of Diomedean help?''

''Bah! Details! I am not an engineer. Engineers I hire. My job is not to do what is impossible, it is to make others do it for me. Only how can I organize things when I am only a more-than-half prisoner of a king who is not interested in meeting my peoples? Hah?''

''Whereas the Lannach tribe is hard pressed and will let you, what they say, write your own ticket. Yes.'' Sandra laughed, with a touch of genuine humor. ''Very good, my friend! Only one question now, how do we get to the Lannachs?''

She waved a hand at their surroundings. It was not an encouraging view.

The *Gerunis* was a typical raft: a big structure, of light tough balsalike logs lashed together with enough open space and flexibility to yield before the sea. A wall of uprights, pegged to the transverse logs, defined a capacious hold and supported a main deck of painfully trimmed planks. Poop and forecastle rose at either end, their flat roofs bearing artillery and, in the former case, the outsize tiller. Between them were seaweed-thatched cabins for storage, workshops, and living quarters. The overall dimensions were about sixty meters by fifteen, tapering toward a false bow which provided a catapult platform and some streamlining. A foremast and mainmast each carried three big square sails, a lateen-rigged mizzen stood just forward of the poop. Given a favoring wind—remembering the force of most winds on this planet—the seemingly awkward craft could make several knots, and even in a dead calm it could be rowed.

It held about a hundred Diomedeans plus wives and children. Of those, ten couples were aristocrats, with private apartments in the poop; twenty were ranking sailors, with special skills, entitled to one room per family in the main-deck cabins; the rest were common deckhands, barracked into the forecastle.

Not far away floated the rest of this squadron. There were rafts of various types, some primarily dwelling units like the *Gerunis,* some triple-decked for cargo, some bearing the long sheds in which fish and seaweed were processed. Often several at a time were linked together, to form a little temporary island. Moored to them, or patrolling between, were the outrigger canoes. Wings beat in the sky, where aerial detachments kept watch for an enemy: full-time professional warriors, the core of Drak'ho's military strength.

Beyond this outlying squadron, the other divisions of

the Fleet darkened the water as far as a man's eyes would reach. Most of them were fishing. It was brutally hard work, where long nets were trolled by muscle power. Nearly all a Drak'ho's life seemed to go to back-bending labor. But out of these fluid fields they were dragging a harvest which leaped and flashed.

"Like fiends they must drive themselves," observed Van Rijn. He slapped the stout rail. "This is tough wood, even when green, and they chew it smooth with stone and glass tools! Some of these fellows I would like to hire, if the union busybodies can be kept away from them."

Sandra stamped her foot. She had not complained at danger of death, cold and discomfort and the drudgery of Tolk's language lessons filtered through Wace. But there are limits. "Either you talk sense, Freeman, or I go somewhere else! I asked you how we get away from here."

"We get rescued by the Lannachska, of course," said Van Rijn. "Or, rather, they come steal us. Yes, so-fashion will be better. Then, if they fail, friend Delp cannot say it is our fault we are so desired by all parties."

Her tall form grew rigid. "What do you mean? How are they to know we are even here?"

"Maybe Tolk will tell them."

"But Tolk is even more a prisoner than we, not?"

"So. However—" Van Rijn rubbed his hands. "We have a little plan made. He is a good head, him. Almost as good as me."

Sandra glared. "And will you deign to tell me how

you plotted with Tolk, under enemy surveillance, when you cannot even speak Drak'ho?"

"Oh, I speak Drak'ho pretty good," said Van Rijn blandly. "Did you not just hear me admit how I eavesdrop on all the palaver aboard? You think just because I make so much trouble, and still sit hours every day taking special instruction from Tolk, it is because I am a dumb old bell who cannot learn so easy? Horse maneuvers! Half the time we mumble together, he is teaching me his own Lannach lingo. Nobody on this raft knows it, so when they hear us say funny noises they think maybe Tolk tries words of Earth language out, ha? They think he despairs of teaching me through Wace and tries himself to pound some Drak'ho in me. Ho, ho, they are bamboozles, by damn! Why, yesterday I told Tolk a dirty joke in Lannachamael. He looked very disgusted. There is proof that poor old Van Rijn is not fat between the ears. We say nothing of the rest of his anatomy."

Sandra stood quiet for a bit, trying to understand what it meant to learn two nonhuman languages simultaneously, one of them forbidden.

"I do not see why Tolk looks disgusted," mused Van Rijn. "It was a good joke. Listen: there was a salesman who traveled on one of the colonial planets, and—"

"I can guess why," interrupted Sandra hastily. "I mean . . . why Tolk did not think it was a funny tale. Er . . . Freeman Wace was explaining it to me the other day. Here on Diomedes they have not the trait of, um, constant sexuality. They breed once each year only, in the tropics. No families in our sense. They would not think our"—she blushed—"our all-year-around interest in these questions was very normal or very polite."

Van Rijn nodded. "All this I know. But Tolk has seen somewhat of the Fleet, and in the Fleet they do have marriage, and get born at any time of year, just like humans."

"I got that impression," she answered slowly, "and it puzzles me. Freeman Wace said the breeding cycle was in their, their heredity. Instinct, or glands, or what it now is called. How *could* the Fleet live differently from what their glands dictate?"

"Well, they do." Van Rijn shrugged massive shoulders. "Maybe we let some scientist worry about it for a thesis later on, hah?"

Suddenly she gripped his arm so he winced. Her eyes were a green blaze. "But you have not said . . . what is to happen? How is Tolk to get word about us to Lannach? What do we do?"

"I have no idea," he told her cheerily. "I play with the ear."

He cocked a beady eye at the pale reddish overcast. Several kilometers away, enormously timbered, bearing what was almost a wooden castle, floated the flagship of all Drak'ho. A swirl of bat wings was lifting from it and streaming toward the *Gerunis*. Faintly down the sky was borne the screech of a blown sea shell.

"But I think maybe we find out quick," finished Van Rijn, "because his rheumatic majesty comes here now to decide about us."

VII

The admiral's household troops, a hundred full-time warriors, landed with beautiful exactness and snapped their weapons to position. Polished stone and oiled leather caught the dull light like sea-blink; the wind of their wings roared across the deck. A purple banner trimmed with scarlet shook loose, and the *Gerunis* crew, respectfully crowded into the rigging and on the forecastle roof, let out a hoarse ritual cheer.

Delp hyr Orikan advanced from the poop and crouched before his lord. His wife, the beautiful Rodonis sa Axollon, and his two young children came behind him, bellies to the deck and wings over eyes. All wore the scarlet sashes and jeweled armbands which were formal dress.

The three humans stood beside Delp. Van Rijn had vetoed any suggestion that they crouch, too. "It is not right for a member of the Polesotechnic League, he should get down on knees and elbows. Anyway I am not built for it.''

Tolk of Lannach sat haughty next to Van Rijn. His wings were tucked into a net and the leash on his neck was held by a husky sailor. His eyes were as bleak and steady on the admiral as a snake's.

And the armed young males who formed a rough honor guard for Delp their captain had something of the same chill in their manner—not toward Syranax, but toward his son, the heir apparent on whom the admiral leaned. Their spears, rakes, tomahawks, and wood-bayoneted blowguns were held in a gesture of total respect: nevertheless, the weapons were held.

Wace thought that Van Rijn's outsize nose must have an abnormal keenness for discord. Only now did he himself sense the tension on which his boss had obviously been counting.

Syranax cleared his throat, blinked, and pointed his muzzle at the humans. ''Which one of you is captain?'' he asked. It was still a deep voice, but it no longer came from the bottom of the lungs, and there was a mucous rattle in it.

Wace stepped forward. His answer was the one Van Rijn had, hastily and without bothering to explain, commanded that he give: ''The other male is our leader, sir. But he does not speak your language very well as yet. I myself still have trouble with it, so we must use this Lannach'ho prisoner to interpret.''

T'heonax scrowled. ''How should he know what you want to say to us?''

"He has been teaching us your language," said Wace. "As you know, sir, foreign tongues are his main task in life. Because of this natural ability, as well as his special experience with us, he will often be able to guess what we may be trying to say when we search for a word."

"That sounds reasonable." Syranax's gray head wove about. "Yes."

"I wonder!" T'heonax gave Delp an ugly look. It was returned in spades.

"So! By damn, now I talk." Van Rijn rolled forward. "My good friend . . . um . . . er . . . *pokker*, what is the word?—my admiral, we, ahem, we talk-um like good brothers—good brothers, is that how I say-um, Tolk?—"

Wace winced. Despite what Sandra had whispered to him, as they were being hustled here to receive the visitors, he found it hard to believe that so ludicrous an accent and grammar were faked.

And why?

Syranax stirred impatiently. "It may be best if we talked through your companion," he suggested.

"Bilge and barnacles!" shouted Van Rijn. "Him? No, no, me talkum talky-talk self. Straight, like, um, er, what-is-your-title. We talk-um like brothers, ha?"

Syranax sighed. But it did not occur to him to overrule the human. An alien aristocrat was still an aristocrat, in the eyes of this caste-ridden society, and as such might surely claim the right to speak for himself.

"I would have visited you before," said the admiral, "but you could not have conversed with me, and there was so much else to do. As they grow more desperate, the Lannach'honai become more dangerous in their raids and ambushes. Not a day goes by that we do not have at least a minor battle."

"Hm-m-m?" Van Rijn counted off the declension-comparison on his fingers. *"Xammagapai* . . . let me see, *xammagan, xammagai* . . . oh, yes. A small fight! I make-um see no fights, old admiral—I mean, honored admiral."

T'heonax bristled. "Watch your tongue, Eart'ho!" he clipped. He had been over frequently to stare at the prisoners, and their sequestered possessions were in his keeping. Little awe remained—but then, Wace decided, T'heonax was not capable of admitting that a being could possibly exist in any way superior to T'heonax.

"And yours, son," murmured Syranax. To Van Rijn: "Oh, they would scarcely venture this far out. I mean our positions on the mainland are constantly harassed."

"Yes," nodded the Terrestrial, rather blankly.

Syranax lay down on the deck in an easy lion-pose. T'heonax remained standing, taut in Delp's presence. "I have, of course, been getting reports about you," went on the admiral. "They are, ah, remarkable. Yes, remarkable. It's alleged you came from the stars."

"Stars, yes!" Van Rijn's head bobbed with imbecilic eagerness. "We from stars. Far far away."

"Is it true also that your people have established an outpost on the other shore of The Ocean?"

Van Rijn went into a huddle with Tolk. The Lannacha put the question into childish words. After several explanations, Van Rijn beamed. "Yes, yes, we from across Ocean. Far far away."

"Will your friends not come in search of you?"

"They look-um, yes, they look-um plenty hard. By Joe! Look-um all over. You treat-um us good or our friends find out and—" Van Rijn broke off, looking dismayed, and conferred again with Tolk.

"I believe the Eart'ho wishes to apologize for tactlessness," explained the Herald dryly.

"It may be a truthful kind of tactlessness," observed Syranax. "If his friends can, indeed, locate him while he is still alive, much will depend on what kind of treatment he received from us. Eh? The problem is, can they find him that soon? What say, Eart'ho?" He pushed the last question out like a spear.

Van Rijn retreated, lifting his hands as if to ward off a blow. "Help!" he whined. "You help-um us, take us home, old admiral . . . honored admiral . . . we go home and pay-um many many fish."

T'heonax murmured in his father's ear: "The truth comes out—not that I haven't suspected as much already. His friends have no measurable chance of finding him before he starves. If they did, he wouldn't be begging us for help. He'd be demanding whatever struck his fancy."

"*I* would have done that in all events," said the admiral. "Our friend isn't very experienced in these matters, eh? Well, it's good to know how easily truth can be squeezed out of him."

"So," said T'heonax contemptuously, not bothering to whisper, "the only problem is, to get some value out of the beasts before they die."

Sandra's breath sucked sharply in. Wace grasped her arm, opened his mouth, and caught Van Rijn's hurried Anglic murmur: "Shut up! Not a word, you bucket head!" Where upon the merchant resumed his timid smile and attitude of straining puzzlement.

"It isn't right!" exploded Delp. "By the Lodestar; sir, these are guests—not enemies—we can't just *use* them!"

"What else would you do?" shrugged T'heonax.

His father blinked and mumbled, as if weighing the arguments for both sides. Something like a spark jumped between Delp and T'heonax. It ran along the ranked lines of *Gerunis* crew-folk and household troopers as an imperceptible tautening, the barest ripple of muscle and forward slant of weapons.

Van Rijn seemed to get the drift all at once. He recoiled operatically, covered his eyes, then went to his knees before Delp. "No, no!" he screamed. "You take-um us home! You help-um us, we help-um you! You remember say how you help-um us if we help-um you!"

"What's this?"

It was a wild-animal snarl from T'heonax. He surged forward. "You've been bargaining with them, have you?"

"What do you mean?" The executive's teeth clashed together, centimeters from T'heonax's nose. His wing-spurs lifted like knives.

"What sort of help were these creatures going to give you?"

"What do you think?" Delp flung the gage into the winds, and crouched waiting.

T'heonax did not quite pick it up. "Some might guess you had ideas of getting rid of certain rivals within the Fleet," he purred.

In the silence which fell across the raft, Wace could hear how the dragon shapes up in the rigging breathed more swiftly. He could hear the creak of timbers and cables, the slap of waves and the low damp mumble of wind. Almost, he heard obsidian daggers being loosened in their sheaths.

If an unpopular prince finds an excuse to arrest a subordinate whom the commoners trust, there are likely going to be men who will fight. It was not otherwise here on Diomedes.

Syranax broke the explosive quiet. "There's some kind of misunderstanding," he said loudly. "Nobody is going to charge anyone with anything on the basis of this wingless creature's gabble. What's the fuss about? What could he possibly do for any of us, anyway?"

"That remains to be seen," answered T'heonax. "But a race which can fly across The Ocean in less than an equinoctail day must know some handy arts."

He whirled on a quivering Van Rijn. With the relish of the inquisitor whose suspect has broken, he said curtly: "Maybe we can get you home somehow if you help us. We are not sure how to get you home. Maybe your stuff can help us get you home. You show us how to use your stuff."

"Oh, yes!" said Van Rijn. He clasped his hands and waggled his head. "Oh, yes, good sir, I do you want-um."

T'heonax clipped an order. A Drak'ho slithered across the deck with a large box. "I've been in charge of these things," explained the heir. "Haven't tried to fool with it, except for a few knives of that shimmery substance—" Momentarily, his eyes glowed with honest enthusiasm. "You've never *seen* such knives, father! They don't hack or grind, they slice! They'll carve seasoned wood!"

He opened the box. The ranking officers forgot dignity and crowded around. T'heonax waved them back. "Give this blubberpot room to demonstrate," he snapped. "Bowmen, blowgunners, cover him from all sides. Be ready to shoot if necessary."

Van Rijn took out a blaster.

"You mean to fight your way clear?" hissed Wace. "You can't!" He tried to step between Sandra and the menace of weapons which suddenly ringed them in. "They'll fill us with arrows before—"

"I know, I know," growled Van Rijn *sotto voce*. "When will you young pridesters learn, just because he is old and lonely, the boss does not yet have teredos in the brain? You keep back, boy, and when trouble breaks loose, hit the deck and dig a hole."

"What? But—"

Van Rijn turned a broad back on him and said in broken Drak'ho, with servile eagerness: "Here a . . . how you call it? . . . thing. It makes fire. It burn-um holes, by Joe."

"A portable flame thrower—that small?" For a moment, an edge of terror sharpened T'heonax's voice.

"I told you," said Delp, "we can gain more by

dealing honorably with them. By the Lodestar, I think we could get them home, too, if we really tried!''

"You might wait till I'm dead, Delp, before taking the Admiralty,'' said Syranax. If he meant it as a joke, it fell like a bomb. The nearer sailors, who heard it, gasped. The household warriors touched their bows and blowguns. Rodonis sa Axollono spread her wings over her children and snarled. Deckhand females, jammed into the forecastle, let out a whimper of half-comprehending fear.

Delp himself steadied matters. "Quiet!" he bawled. "Belay there! Calm down! By all the devils in the Rainy Stars, have these creatures driven us crazy?''

"See," chattered Van Rijn, "take *blaster* . . . we call-um *blaster* . . . pull-um here—''

The ion beam stabbed out and crashed into the mainmast. Van Rijn yanked it away at once, but it had already made a gouge centimeters deep in that tough wood. Its blue-white flame licked across the deck, whiffed a coiled cable into smoke, and took a section out of the rail, before he released the trigger.

The Drak'honai roared!

It was minutes before they had settled back into the shrouds or onto the decks; curiosity seekers from nearby craft still speckled the sky. However, they were technologically sophisticated in their way. They were excited rather than frightened.

"Let me see that!" T'heonax snatched at the gun.

"Wait, Wait, good sir, wait." Van Rijn snapped open the chamber, in a set of movements screened by his thick hands, and popped out the charge. "Make-um safe first. There."

T'hoeonax turned it over and over. "What a weapon!" he breathed. "What a *weapon!*"

Standing there in a frosty sweat, waiting for Van Rijn to spoon up whatever variety of hell he was cooking, Wace still managed to reflect that the Drak'honai were overestimating. Natural enough, of course. But a gun of this sort would only have a serious effect on ground-fighting tactics—and the old sharper was coolly disarming all the blasters anyway, no uninstructed Diomedean was going to get any value from them—

"I make safe," Van Rijn burbled. "One, two, three, four, five I make safe. . . . Four? Five? Six?" He began turning over the piled-up clothes, blankets, heaters, campstove, and other equipment. "Where other three blasters?"

"What other three?" T'heonax stared at him.

"We have six." Van Rijn counted carefully on his fingers. "*Ja*, six. I give-um all to good sir Delp here."

"WHAT?"

Delp leaped at the human, cursing. "That's a lie! There were only three, and you've got them there!"

"Help!" Van Rijn scuttled behind T'heonax. Delp's body clipped the admiral's son. Both Drak'honai went over in a whirl of wings and tails.

"*He's plotting mutiny!*" screamed T'heonax.

Wace threw Sandra to the deck and himself above her. The air grew dense with missiles.

Van Rijn turned ponderously to grab the sailor in

charge of Tolk. But that Drak'ho had already sprung away to Delp's defense. Van Rijn had only to peel off the imprisoning net.

"Now," he said in fluent Lannachamael, "go bring an army to fetch us out of here. Quick, before someone notices!"

The Herald nodded, threshed his wings, and was gone into a sky where battle ran loose.

Van Rijn stooped over Wace and Sandra. "This way," he panted under the racket. A chance tail-buffet, as a sailor fought two troopers, brought a howl from him. "Thunder and lightning! Pest and poison ivy!" He wrestled Sandra to her feet and hustled her toward the comparative shelter of the forecastle.

When they stood inside its door, among terrified females and cubs, looking out at the fight, he said:

"It is a pity that Delp will go under. He has no chance. He is a decent sort; we could maybe have done business."

"All saints in Heaven!" choked Wace. "You touched off a civil war just to get your messenger away?"

"You know perhaps a better method?" asked Van Rijn.

VIII

When Commander Krakna fell in battle against the
invaders, the Flock's General Council picked one
Trolwen to succeed him. They were the elders, and
their choice comparatively youthful, but the Lannachska thought it only natural to be led by young
males. A commander needed the physical stamina of
two, to see them through a hard and dangerous migration every year; he seldom lived to grow feeble. Any
rash impulses of his age were curbed by the General
Council itself, the clan leaders who had grown too old
to fly at the head of their squadron-septs and not yet so
old and weak as to be left behind on some winter
journey.

Trolwen's mother belonged to the Trekkhan group, a
distinguished bloodline with rich properties on Lan-

nach; she herself had added to that wealth by shrewd trading. She guessed that his father was Tornak of the Wendru—not that she cared especially, but Trolwen looked noticeably like that fierce warrior. However, it was his own record as a clan-elected officer, in storm and battle and negotiation and everyday routine, which caused the Council to pick him as leader of all the clans. In the ten-days since, he had been the chief of a losing cause; but possibly his folk were pressed back into the uplands more slowly than would have happened without him.

Now he led a major part of the Flock's fighting strength out against the Fleet itself.

Vernal equinox was barely past, but already the days lengthened with giant strides; each morning the sun rose farther north, and a milder air melted the snows until Lannach's dales were a watery brawling. It took only one hundred thirty days from equinox to Last Sunrise—thereafter, during the endless light of High Summer, there would be nothing but rain or mist to cover an attack.

And if the Drakska were not whipped by autumn, reflected Trolwen grimly, there would be no point in trying further; the Flock would be done.

His wings thrust steadily at the sky, the easy strength-hoarding beat of a wanderer born. Under him there was a broken white mystery of cloud, with the sea far beneath it peering through in a glimmer like polished glass; overhead lay a clear violet-blue roof, the night and the stars. Both moons were up, hasty Flichtan driving from horizon to horizon in a day and a half, Nua so much slower that her phases moved more rapidly than herself. He drew the cold, flowing darkness into his lungs, felt the thrust in muscles and the ripple in fur, but without the sensuous enjoyment of an ordinary flight.

He was thinking too hard about killing.

A commander should not show indecision, but he was young and gray Tolk the Herald would understand. "How shall we know that these beings are on the same raft as when you left?" he asked. He spoke in the measured, breath-conserving rhythm of a route flight. The wind muttered beneath his words.

"We cannot be sure, of course, Flockchief," replied Tolk. "But the fat one considered that possibility, too. He said he would manage, somehow, to be out on deck in plain view every day just at sunrise."

"Perhaps, though," worried Trolwen, "the Draka authorities will have locked him away, suspecting his help in your escape."

"What he did was probably not noticed in all the turmoil," said Tolk.

"And perhaps he cannot help us after all." Trolwen shivered. The Council had spoken strongly against this raid: too risky, too many certain casualties. The turbulent clans had roared their own disapproval. He had had difficulty persuading them all.

And if it turned out he was throwing away lives on something as grotesque as this, for no good purpose— Trolwen was as patriotic as any young male whose folk have been cruelly attacked; but he was not unconcerned about his own future. It had happened in the past that commanders who failed badly were read forever out of the Flock, like any common thief or murderer.

He flew onward.

A chill thin light had been stealing into the sky for a time. Now the higher clouds began to flush red, and a gleam went over the half-hidden sea. It was crucial to reach the Fleet at just about this moment, enough light to see what to do and not enough to give the enemy ample warning.

A Whistler, with the slim frame and outsize wings of adolescence, emerged from a fog-bank. The shrill notes of his lips carried far and keenly. Tolk, who as Chief Herald headed the education of these messenger-scouts, cocked his head and nodded. "We guessed it very well," he said calmly. "The rafts are only five buaska ahead."

"So I hear." Tension shook Trolwen's voice. "Now—"

He broke off. More of the youths were beating up-wind into view, faster than an adult could fly. Their whistles wove into an exuberant battle music. Trolwen read the code like his own speech, clamped jaws together, and waved a hand at his standard bearer. Then he dove.

As he burst through the clouds, he saw the Fleet spread enormous, still far below him but covering the waters, from those islands called The Pups to the rich eastern driss banks. Decks and decks and decks cradled on a purplish-gray calm, masts raked upward like teeth, the dawn-light smote the admiral's floating castle and burned off his banner. There was an explosion skyward from rafts and canoes, as the Drak'honai heard the yells of their own sentries and went to arms.

Trolwen folded his wings and stooped. Behind him, in a wedge of clan-squadrons, roared three thousand Lannacha males. Even as he fell, he glared in search —where was that double-cursed Eart'a monster —*there!* The distance-devouring vision of a flying animal picked out three ugly shapes on a raft's quarterdeck, waving and jumping about.

Trolwen spread his wings to brake. "Here!" he cried. The standard bearer glided to a stop, hovered, and unfurled the red flag of Command. The squadrons changed from wedge to battle formation, peeled off, and dove for the raft.

The Drakska were forming their own ranks with terrifying speed and discipline. "All smoke-snuffing gods!" groaned Trolwen. "If we could just have used a single squadron—a raid, not a full-scale battle—"

"A single squadron could hardly have brought the Eart'ska back alive, Flockchief," said Tolk. "Not from the very core of the enemy. We have to make it seem . . . not worth their while . . . to keep up the engagement, when we retreat."

"They know ghostly well what we've come for," said Trolwen. "Look how they swarm to that raft!"

The Flock troop had now punched through a shaken line of Draka patrols and reached water surface. One detachment attacked the target vessel, landed in a ring around the humans and then struck out to seize the entire craft. The rest stayed air-borne to repel the enemy's counter-assault.

It was simple, clumsy ground fighting on deck. Both sides were similarly equipped: weapon technology seems to diffuse faster than any other kind. Wooden swords set with chips of flint, fire-hardened spears, clubs, daggers, tomahawks, struck small wicker shields and leather harness. Tails smacked out, talons ripped, wings buffeted and cut with horny spurs, teeth closed in throats, fists battered on flesh. Hard-pressed, a male would fly upward—there was little attempt to keep ranks, it was a free-for-all. Trolwen had no special interest in that phase of the battle; having landed superior numbers, he knew he could take the raft, if only his aerial squadrons could keep the remaining Drakska off.

He thought—conventionally, in the wake of a thousand bards—how much like a dance a battle in the air was: intricate, beautiful, and terrible. To co-ordinate the efforts of a thousand or more warriors a-wing reached the highest levels of art.

The backbone of such a force was the archers. Each gripped a bow as long as himself in his foot talons, drew the cord with both hands and let fly, plucked a fresh arrow from the belly quiver with his teeth and had it ready to nook before the string snapped taut. Such a corps, trained almost from birth, could lay down a curtain which none might cross alive. But after the whistling death was spent, as it soon was, they must stream back to the bearers for more arrows. That was the most vulnerable aspect of their work, and the rest of the army existed to guard it.

Some cast bolas, some the heavy sharp-edged

boomerang, some the weighted net in which a wing-tangled foe could plunge to his death. Blowguns were a recent innovation, observed among foreign tribes in the tropical meeting places. Here the Drakska were ahead: their guns had a bolt-operated repeater mechanism and fire-hardened wooden bayonets. Also, the separate military units in the Fleet were more tightly organized.

On the other hand, they still relied on an awkward set of horn calls to integrate their entire army. Infinitely more flexible, the Whistler corps darted from leader to leader, weaving the Flock into one great wild organism.

Up and down the battle ramped, while the sun rose and the clouds broke apart and the sea grew red-stained. Trolwen clipped his orders: Hunlu to reinforce the upper right flank, Torcha to feint at the admiral's raft while Srygen charged on the opposite wing—

But the Fleet was here, thought Trolwen bleakly, with all its arsenals: more missiles than his fliers, who were outnumbered anyway, could ever have carried. If this fight wasn't broken off soon—

The raft with the Eart'ska had now been seized. Draka canoes were approaching to win it back. One of them opened up with fire weapons: the dreaded, irresistible burning oil of the Fleet, pumped from a ceramic nozzle; catapults throwing vases of the stuff which exploded in gouts of flame on impact. Those were the weapons which had annihilated the boats owned by the Flock, and taken its coastal towns. Trolwen cursed with a reflex anguish when he saw.

But the Eart'ska were off the raft, six strong porters carrying each one in a specially woven net. By changing bearers often, those burdens could be taken to the Flock's mountain stronghold. The food boxes, hastily dragged up from the hold, were less difficult—one porter to each. A Whistler warbled success.

"Let's go!" Orders rattled from Trolwen, his messengers swooped to the appropriate squadrons. "Hunlu and Srygen, close ranks about the bearers; Dwarn fly above with half his command, the other half guard the left wing. Rearguards—"

The morning was perceptibly further along before he had disengaged. His nightmare had been that the larger Fleet forces would pursue. A running battle all the way home could have snapped the spine of his army. But as soon as he was plainly in retreat, the enemy broke contact and retired to decks.

"As you predicted, Tolk," panted Trolwen.

"Well, Flockchief," said the Herald with his usual calm, "they themselves wouldn't be anxious for such a melee. It would over-extend them, leave their rafts virtually defenseless—for all they know, your whole idea was to lure them into such a move. So they have merely decided that the Eart'ska aren't worth the trouble and risk: an opinion which the Eart'ska themselves must have been busily cultivating in them."

"Let's hope it's not a correct belief. But however the gods decree, Tolk . . . you still foresaw this outcome. Maybe you should be Commander."

"Oh, no. Not I. It was the fat Eart'ska who predicted this—in detail."

Trolwen laughed. "Perhaps, then, he should command."

"Perhaps," said Tolk, very thoughtfully, "he will."

IX

The northern coast of Lannach sloped in broad valleys
to the Sea of Achan; and here, in game-filled forests
and on grassy downs, had arisen those thorps in which
the Flock's clans customarily dwelt. Where Sagna Bay
made its deep cut into the land, many such hamlets had
grown together into larger units. Thus the towns came
to be Ulwen and flinty Mannenach and Yo of the
Carpenters.

But their doors were broken down and their roofs
burned open; Drak'ho canoes lay on Sagna's beaches,
Dark'ho war-bands laired in empty Ulwen and pa-
trolled the Anch Forest and rounded up the hornbeast
herds emerging from winter sleep on Duna Brae.

Its boats sunk, its houses taken, and its hunting and
fishing grounds cut off, the Flock retired into the up-

lands. On the quaking lava slopes of Mount Oborch or in the cold canyons of the Misty Mountains, there were a few small settlements where the poorer clans had lived. The females, the very old and the very young could be crowded into these; tents could be pitched and caves occupied. By scouring this gaunt country from Hark Heath to the Ness, and by going often hungry, the whole Flock could stay alive for a while longer.

But the heart of Lannach was the north coast, which the Drak'honai now forbade. Without it, the Flock was nothing, a starveling tribe of savages . . . until autumn, when Birthtime would leave them altogether helpless.

"It is not well," said Trolwen inadequately.

He strode up a narrow trail, toward the village— what was its name now? Salmenbrok—which perched on the jagged crest above. Beyond that, dark volcanic rock still streaked with snowfields climbed dizzily upward to a crater hidden in its own vapors. The ground shivered underfoot, just a bit, and van Rijn heard a rumble in the guts of the planet.

Poor isostatic balance . . . to be expected under these low-density conditions . . . a geologic history of overly-rapid change, earthquake, eruption, flood, and new lands coughed up from the sea bottom in a mere thousand decades . . . hence, in spite of all the water, a catastrophically uneven climate— He wrapped the stinking fur blanket they had given him more closely around his rough-coated frame, blew on numbed hands, peered into the damp sky for a glimpse of sun, and swore.

This was no place for a man his age and girth. He should be at home, in his own deeply indented armchair, with a good cigar, a tall drink and the gardens of Jakarta flaming around him. For a moment, the remembrance of Earth was so sharp that he snuffled in self-pity. It was bitter to leave his bones in this nightmare land, when he had thought to pull Earth's soft green turf about his weary body. . . . Hard and cruel, yes, and every day the company must be getting deeper into the red ink without him there to oversee! That hauled him back to practicalities.

"Let me get this all clear in my head," he requested. He found himself rather more at home in Lannachamael than he had been—even without faking—in the Drak'ho speech. Here, by chance, the grammar and the guttural noises were not too far from his mother tongue. Already he approached fluency.

"You came back from your migration and found the enemy was here waiting for you?" he continued.

Trolwen jerked his head in a harsh and painful gesture. "Yes. Hitherto we had only known vaguely of their existence; their home regions are well to the southeast of ours. We knew they had been forced to leave because suddenly the trech—the fish which are the mainstay of their diet—had altered their own habits, shifting from Draka waters to Achan. But we had no idea the Fleet was bound for our country."

Van Rijn's long hair swished, lank and greasy-black, the careful curls all gone out of it, as he nodded. "It is like home history. In the Middle Ages on Earth, when the herring changed their ways for some begobbled herring reason, it would change the history of maritime countries. Kings would fall, by damn, and wars would be fought over the new fishing grounds.''

''It has never been of great importance to us,'' said Trolwen. ''A few clans in the Sagna region have . . . had small dugouts, and got much of their food with hook and line. None of this beast-labor the Draks-ka go through, dragging those nets, even if they do pull in more fish! But for our folk generally, it was a minor thing. To be sure, we were pleased, several years ago, when the trech appeared in great numbers in the Sea of Achan. It is large and tasty, its oil and bones have many uses. But it was not such an occasion for rejoicing as if oh, as if the wild hornbeasts had doubled their herds overnight.''

His fingers closed convulsively on the handle of his tomahawk. He was, after all, quite young. ''Now I see the gods sent the trech to us in anger and mockery. For the Fleet followed the trech.''

Van Rijn paused on the trail, wheezing till he drowned out the distant lava rumbles. ''Whoof! Hold it there, you! Not so like a God-forgotten horse race, if you please—Ah. If the fish are not so great for you, why not let the Fleet have the Achan waters?''

It was, he knew, not a true question: only a stimulus. Trolwen delivered himself of several explosive obscenities before answering, ''They attacked us the moment we came home this spring. They had already occupied our coastlands! And even had they not done so, would you let a powerful horde of . . . strangers whose very habits are alien and evil . . . would you let them dwell at your windowsill? How long could such an arrangement last?''

Van Rijn nodded again. Just suppose a nation with tyrant government and filthy personal lives were to ask for the Moon, on the grounds that they needed it and it was not of large value to Earth—

Personally, he could afford to be tolerant. In many ways, the Drak'honai were closer to the human norm than the Lannachska. Their masterserf culture was a natural consequence of economics: given only neolithic tools, a raft big enough to support several families represented an enormous capital investment. It was simply not possible for disgruntled individuals to strike out on their own; they were at the mercy of the State. In such cases, power always concentrates in the hands of aristocratic warriors and intellectual priesthoods; among the Drak'honai, those two classes had merged into one.

The Lannachska, on the other hand—more typically Diomedean—were primarily hunters. They had very few highly specialized craftsmen; the individual could survive using tools made by himself. The low calorie/area factor of a hunting economy made them spread out thin over a large region, each small group nearly independent of the rest. They exerted themselves in spasms, during the chase for instance; but they did not have to toil day after day until they nearly dropped, as the common netman or oarsman or deckhand must in the Fleet—hence there was no economic justification on Lannach for a class of bosses and overseers.

Thus, their natural political unit was the little matrilineal clan. Such semiformal blood groups, almost free of government, were rather loosely organized into the Great Flock. And the Flock's *raison d'être*—apart from minor inter-sept business at home—was simply to increase the safety of all when every Diomedean on Lannach flew south for the winter.

Or came home to war!

"It is interesting," murmured Van Rijn, half in Anglic. "Among our peoples, like on most planets, only the agriculture folk got civilized. Here they make no farms at all: the big half-wild hornbeast herds is closest thing, *nie?* You hunt, berrypick, reap wild grain, fish a little—yet some of you know writing and make books; I see you have machines and houses, and weave cloth. Could be, the every-year stimulus of meeting foreigners in the tropics gives you ideas?"

"What?" asked Trolwen vaguely.

"Nothings. I just wondered, me, why—since life here is easy enough so you have time for making civilization—you do not grow so many you eat up all your game and chop down all your woods. That is what we called a successful civilization back on Earth."

"Our numbers do not increase fast," said Trolwen. "About three hundred years ago, a daughter Flock was formed and moved elsewhere, but the increase is very slow. We lose so many on the migrations, you see— storm, exhaustion, sickness, barbarian attack, wild animals, sometimes cold or famine—" He hunched his wings, the Diomedean equivalent of a shrug.

"Ah-ha! Natural selection. Which is all well and good, if nature is obliging to pick you for survival. Otherwise gives awful noises about tragedy." Van

Rijn stroked his goatee. The chins beneath it were getting bristly as his last application of antibeard enzyme wore off. "So. It does give one notion of what made your race get brains. Hibernate or migrate! And if you migrate, then be smart enough to meet all kinds trouble, by damn."

He resumed his noisy walk up the trail. "But we got our troubles of now to think about, especially since they are too the troubles belonging with Nicholas van Rijn. Which is not to be stood. Hmpf! Well, now, tell me more. I gather the Fleet scrubbed its decks with you and kicked you up here where the only flat country is the map. You want home to the lowlands again. You also want to get rid of the Fleet."

"We gave them a good fight," said Trolwen stiffly. "We still can—and will, by my grandmother's ghost! There were reasons why we were defeated so badly. We came tired and hungry back from ten-days of flight; one is always weak at the end of the springtime journey home. Our strongholds had already been occupied. The Draka flamethrowers set afire such other defenses as we contrived, and made it impossible for us to fight them on the water, where their real strength lies."

His teeth snapped together in a carnivore reflex. "And we have to overcome them soon! If we don't we are finished. And they know it!"

"I am not clear over this yet," admitted Van Rijn. "The hurry is that all your young are born the same time, *nie?*"

"Yes." Trolwen topped the rise and waited beneath the walls of Salmenbrok for his puffing guest.

Like all Lannachska settlements, it was fortified

against enemies, animal or intelligent. There was no stockade—that would be pointless here where all the higher life-forms had wings. An average building was roughly in the shape of an ancient Terrestrial block-house. The ground floor was doorless and had mere slits for windows; entrance was through an upper story or a trap in the thatched roof. A hamlet was fortified not by outer walls but by being woven together with covered bridges and underground passages.

Up here, above timberline, the houses were of undressed stone mortared in place, rather than the logs more common among the valley clans. But this thorp was solidly made, furnished with a degree of comfort that indicated how bountiful the lowlands must be.

Van Rijn took time to admire such features as wooden locks constructed like Chinese puzzles, a wooden lathe set with a cutting edge of painstakingly fractured diamond, and a wooden saw whose teeth were of renewable volcanic glass. A communal windmill ground nuts and wild grain, as well as powering numerous smaller machines; it included a pump which filled a great stone basin in the overhanging cliff with water, and the water could be let down again to keep the mill turning when there was no wind. He even saw a tiny sail-propelled railroad, with wooden-wheeled basketwork carts running on iron-hard wooden rails. It carried flint and obsidian from the local quarries, timber from the forests, dried fish from the coast, furs and herbs from the lowlands, handicrafts from all the island. Van Rijn was delighted.

"So!" he said. "Commerce! You are fundamentally capitalists. Ha, by damn, I think soon we do some business!"

Trolwen shrugged. "There is nearly always a strong wind up here. Why should we not let it take our burdens? Actually, all the apparatus you see took many lifetimes to complete—we're not like those Drakska, wearing themselves out with labor."

Salmenbrok's temporary population crowded about the human, with mumbling and twittering and wing-flapping, the cubs twisting around his legs and their mothers shrieking at them to come back. "Ten thousand purple devils!" he choked. "They think maybe I am a politician to kiss their brats, ha?"

"Come this way," said Trolwen. "Toward the Males' Temple—females and young may not follow, they have their own." He led the way along another path, making an elaborate salute to a small idol in a niche on the trail. From its crudity, the thing had been carved centuries ago. The Flock seemed to have only a rather incoherent polytheism for religion, and not to take that very seriously these days; but it was as strict about ritual and tradition as some classic British regiment—which, in many ways, it resembled.

Van Rijn trudged after, casting a glance behind. The females here looked little different from those in the Fleet: a bit smaller and slimmer than the males, their wings larger but without a fully developed spur. In fact, racially the two folk seemed identical.

And yet, if all that the company's agents had learned

about Diomedes was not pure gibberish, the Drak'honai represented a biological monstrousness. An impossibility!

Trolwen followed the man's curious gaze, and sighed. "You can notice nearly half our nubile females are expecting their next cub."

"Hm-m-m. *Ja*, there is your problem. Let me see if I understand it right. Your young are all born at the fall equinox—"

"Yes. Within a few days of each other; the exceptions are negligible."

"But it is not so many ten-days thereafter you must leave for the south. Surely a new baby cannot fly?"

"Oh, no. It clings to the mother all the way; it is born with arms able to grasp hard. There is no cub from the preceding year; a nursing female does not get pregnant. Her two-year-old is strong enough to fly the distance, given rest periods in which it rides on someone's back—though that's the age group where we suffer the most loss. Three-year-olds and above need only be guided and guarded: their wings are quite adequate."

"But this makes much trouble for the mother, not so?"

"She is assisted by the half-grown clan members, or the old who are past childbearing but not yet too old to survive the journey. And the males, of course, do all the hunting, scouting, fighting, and so forth."

"So. You come to the south. I hear told it makes easy to live there, nuts and fruits and fish to scoop from the water. Why do you come back?"

"This is our home," said Trolwen simply.

After a moment: "And, of course, the tropic islands could never support all the myriads which gather there each midwinter—twice a year, actually. By the time the migrants are ready to leave, they have eaten that country bare."

"I see. Well, keep on. In the south, at solstice time, is when you rut."

"Yes. The desire comes on us—but you know what I mean."

"Of course," said Van Rijn blandly.

"And there are festivals, and trading with the other tribes . . . frolic or fight—" The Lannacha sighed. "Enough. Soon after solstice, we return, arriving here sometime before equinox, when the large animals on which we chiefly depend have awoken from their winter sleep and put on a little flesh. There you have the pattern of our lives, Eart'ho."

"It sounds like fun, if I was not too old and fat." Van Rijn blew his nose lugubriously. "Do not get old, Trolwen. It is so lonesome. You are lucky, dying on migration when you grow feeble, you do not live wheezy and helpless with nothing but your dear memories, like me."

"I'm not likely to get old as matters stand now," said Trolwen.

"When your young are born, all at once in the fall *ja*," mused Van Rijn, "I can see how then is time for nothing much but obstetrics. And if you have not food and shelter and such helps all ready, most of the young die—"

"They are replaceable." said Trolwen, with a degree of casualness that showed he was, after all, not just a man winged and tailed. His tone sharpened. "But the females who bear them are more vital to our strength. A recent mother must be properly rested and fed, you understand, or she will never reach the south—and consider what a part of our total numbers are going to become mothers. It's a question of the Flock's survival as a nation! And those filthy Drakska, breeding all the year round like . . . like fish. . . . *No!*"

"No indeed," said Van Rijn. "Best we think of somethings very fast, or I grow very hungry, too."

"I spent lives to rescue you," said Trolwen, "because we all hoped you would think of something yourself."

"Well," said Van Rijn, "the problem is to get word to my own people at Thursday Landing. Then they come here quick, by damn, and I will tell them to clean up on the Fleet."

Trolwen smiled. Even allowing for the unhuman shape of his mouth, it was a smile without warmth or humor. "No, no," he said. "Not that easily. I dare not, cannot spare the folk, or the time and effort, in some crazy attempt to cross The Ocean . . . not while Drak-'ho has us by the throat. Also—forgive me—how do I know that you will be interested in helping us, once you are able to go home again?"

He looked away from his companion, toward the porticoed cave that was the Males' Temple. Steam rolled from its mouth, there was the hiss of a geyser within.

"I myself might have decided otherwise," he added

abruptly, in a very low voice. "But I have only limited powers—any plan of mine—the Council—do you see? The Council is suspicious of three wingless monsters. It thinks . . . we know so little about you . . . our only sure hold on you is your own desperation . . . the Council will allow no help to be brought for you until the war is over."

Van Rijn lifted his shoulders and spread his hands. "Confidential, Trolwen, boy, in their place I would do the same."

X

Now darkness waned. Soon there would be light nights, when the sun hovered just under the sea and the sky was like white blossoms. Already both moons could be seen in full phase after sunset. As Rodonis stepped from her cabin, swift Sk'huanax climbed the horizon and swung up among the many stars toward slow and patient Lykaris. Between them, She Who Waits and He Who Pursues cast a shuddering double bridge over broad waters.

Rodonis was born to the old nobility, and had been taught to smile at Moons worship. Good enough for the common sailors, who would otherwise go back to their primitive bloody sacrifices to Aeak'ha-in-the-Deeps, but really, an educated person knew there was only the Lodestar. . . . Nevertheless, Rodonis went down on the deck, hooded herself with her wings, and whispered her trouble to bright mother Lykaris.

"A song do I pledge you, a song all for yourself, to be made by the Fleet's finest bards and sung in your honor when next you hold wedding with He Who Pursues you. You will not wed Him again for more than a year, the astrologues tell me; there will be time enough to fashion a song for you which shall live while the Fleet remains afloat, O Lykaris: if but you will spare me my Delp."

She did not address Sk'huanax the Warrior, any more than a male Drak'ho would have dreamed of petitioning the Mother. But she said to Lykaris in her mind, that there could be no harm in calling to his attention the fact the Delp was a brave person who had never omitted the proper offerings.

The moons brightened. A bank of cloud in the west bulked like frosty mountains. Far off stood the ragged loom of an island, and she could hear pack ice cough in the north. It was a big strange seascape, this was not the dear green Southwater whence starvation had driven the Fleet and she wondered if Achan's gods would ever let the Drak'honai call it home.

The *lap-lap* of waves, creaking timbers, cables that sang as the dew tauntened them, wind-mumble in shrouds, a slatting sail, the remote plaintiveness of a flute and the nearer homely noises from this raft's own forecastle, snores and cub-whimpers and some couple's satisfied grunt . . . were a strong steady comfort in this cold emptiness named Achan Sea. She thought of her own young, two small furry shapes in a richly tapestried bed, and it gave her the remaining strength needed. She spread her wings and mounted the air.

From above, the Fleet at night was all clumps of shadow, with the rare twinkle of firepots where some crew worked late. Most were long abed, worn out from a day of dragging nets, manning sweeps and capstans, cleaning and salting and pickling the catch, furling and unfurling the heavy sails of the rafts, harvesting driss and fruitweed, felling trees and shaping timber with stone tools. A common crew member, male or female, had little in life except hard brutal labor. Their recreations were almost as coarse and violent: the dances, the athletic contests, the endless lovemaking, the bawdy songs roared out from full lungs over a barrel of seagrain beer.

For a moment, as such thoughts crossed her mind, Rodonis felt pride in her crewfolk. To the average noble, a commoner was a domestic animal, ill-mannered, unlettered, not quite decent, to be kept in line by whip and hook for his own good. But flying over the great sleeping beast of a Fleet, Rodonis sensed its sheer vigor, coiled like a snake beneath her—these were the lords of the sea, and Drak'ho's haughty banners were raised on the backs of Drak'ho's lusty deckhands.

Perhaps it was simply that her own husband's ancestors had risen from the forecastle not many generations back. She had seen him help his crew often enough, working side by side with them in storm or fish run; she had learned it was no disgrace to swing a quernstone or set up a massive loom for herself.

If labor was pleasing to the Lodestar, as the holy books said, then why should Drak'ho nobles consider it distasteful? There was something bloodless about the old families, something not quite healthy. They died out, to be replaced from below, century after century. It was well-known that deckhands had the most offspring, skilled handicrafters and full-time warriors rather less, hereditary officers fewest of all. Why, Admiral Syranax had in a long life begotten only one son and two daughters. She, Rodonis, had two cubs already, after a mere four years of marriage.

Did this not suggest that the high Lodestar favored the honest person working with honest hands?

But no . . . those Lannach'honai all had young every other year, like machinery, even though many of the tykes died on migration. And the Lannach'honai did not work: not really: they hunted, herded, fished with their effeminate hooks, they were vigorous enough but they never stuck to a job through hours and days like a Drak'ho sailor . . . and, of course, their habits were just disgusting. *Animal!* A couple of ten-days a year, down in the twilight of equatorial solstice, indiscriminate lust, and that was all. For the rest of your life, the father of your cub was only another male to you—not that you knew who he was anyway, you hussy!—and at home there was no modesty between the sexes, there wasn't even much distinction in everyday habits, because there was no more desire. Ugh!

Still, those filthy Lannach'honai had flourished, so maybe the Lodestar did not care. . . . No, it was too cold a thought, here in the night wind under ashen

Sk'huanax. Surely the Lodestar had appointed the Fleet an instrument, to destroy those Lannach beasts and take the country they had been defiling.

Rodonis' wings beat a little faster. The flagship was close now, its turrets like mountain peaks in the dark. There were many lamps burning, down on deck or in shuttered rooms. There were warriors cruising endlessly above and around. The admiral's flag was still at the masthead, so he had not yet died; but the death watch thickened hour by hour.

Like carrion birds waiting, thought Rodonis with a shudder.

One of the sentries whistled her to a hover and flapped close. Moonlight glistened on his polished spearhead. "Hold! Who are you?"

She had come prepared for such a halt, but briefly, the tongue clove to her mouth. For she was only a female, and a monster laired beneath her.

A gust of wind rattled the dried things hung from a yardarm: the wings of some offending sailor who now sat leashed to an oar or a millstone, if he still lived. Rodonis thought of Delp's back bearing red stumps, and her anger broke loose in a scream:

"Do you speak in that tone to a sa Axollon?"

The warrior did not know her personally, among the thousands of Fleet citizens, but he knew an officer-class scarf; and it was plain to see that a life's toil had never been allowed to twist this slim-flanked body.

"Down on the deck, scum!" yelled Rodonis. "Cover your eyes when you address me!"

"I . . . my lady," he stammered, "I did not—"

She dove directly at him. He had no choice but to get out of the way. Her voice cracked whip-fashion, trailing her: "Assuming, of course, that your boatswain has first obtained my permission for you to speak to me."

"But ...but ...but—" Other fighting males had come now, to wheel as helplessly in the air. Such laws did exist; no one had enforced them to the letter for centuries, but—

An officer on the main deck met the situation when Rodonis landed. "My lady," he said with due deference, "it is not seemly for an unescorted female to be abroad at all, far less to visit this raft of sorrow."

"It is necessary," she told him. "I have a word for Captain T'heonax which will not wait."

"The captain is at his honored father's bunkside, my lady. I dare not—"

"Let it be your teeth he has pulled, then, when he learns that Rodonis sa Axollon could have forestalled another mutiny!"

She flounced across the deck and leaned on the rail, as if brooding her anger above the sea. The officer gasped. It was like a tail-blow to the stomach. "My lady! At once . . . wait, wait here, only the littlest of moments—Guard! Guard, there! Watch over my lady. See that she lacks not." He scuttled off.

Rodonis waited. Now the real test was coming.

There had been no problem so far. The Fleet was too shaken; no officer, worried ill, would have refused her demand when she spoke of a second uprising.

The first had been bad enough. Such a horror, an actual revolt against the Lodestar's own Oracle, had been unknown for more than a hundred years . . . and with a war to fight at the same time! The general impulse had been to deny that anything serious had happened at all. A regrettable misunderstanding Delp's folk misled, fighting their gallant, hopeless fight out of loyalty to their captain . . . after all, you couldn't expect ordinary sailors to understand the more modern principle, that the Fleet and its admiral transcended any individual raft—

Harshly, her tears at the time only a dry memory, Rodonis rehearsed her interview with Syranax, days ago.

"I am sorry, my lady," he had said. "Believe me I am sorry. Your husband was provoked, and he had more justice on his side than T'heonax. In fact, I know it was just a fight which happened, not planned, only a chance spark touching off old grudges, and my own son mostly to blame."

"Then let your son suffer for it!" she had cried.

The gaunt old skull wove back and forth, implacably. "No. He may not be the finest person in the world, but he is my son. And the heir. I haven't long to live, and wartime is no time to risk a struggle over the succession. For the Fleet's sake, T'heonax must succeed me without argument from anyone; and for this, he must have an officially unstained record."

"But why can't you let Delp go too?"

"By the Lodestar, if I could! But it's not possible. I can give everyone else amnesty, yes, and I will. But there must be one to bear the blame, one on whom to vent the pain of our hurts. Delp has to be accused of

engineering a mutiny, and be punished, so that every-
body else can say, 'Well, we fought each other, but
it was all his fault, so now we can trust each other
again.' "

The admiral sighed, a tired breath out of shrunken
lungs. "I wish to the Lodestar I didn't have to do this. I
wish . . . I'm fond of you too, my lady. I wish we
could be friends again."

"We can," she whispered, "if you will set Delp
free."

The conqueror of Maion looked bleakly at her and
said: "No. And now I have heard enough."

She had left his presence.

And the days passed, and there was the farcical
nightmare of Delp's trial, and the nightmare of the
sentence passed on him, and the nightmare of waiting
for its execution. The Lannach'ho raid had been like a
moment's waking from feverdreams: for it was sharp
and real, and your shipmate was no longer your
furtive-eyed enemy but a warrior who met the barbarian
in the clouds and whipped him home from your cubs!

Three nights afterward, Admiral Syranax lay dying.
Had he not fallen sick, Delp would now be a mutilated
slave, but in this renewed tension and uncertainty, so
controversial a sentence was naturally stayed.

Once T'heonax had the Admiralty, thought Rodonis
in a cold corner of her brain, there would be no more
delay. Unless—

"Will my lady come this way?"

They were obsequious, the officers who guided her
across the deck and into the great gloomy pile of logs.

Household servants, pattering up and down window-less corridors by lamplight, stared at her in a kind of terror. Somehow, the most secret things were always known to the forecastle, immediately, as if smelled.

It was dark in here, stuffy, and silent. *So* silent. The sea is never still. Only now did Rodonis realize that she had not before, in all her life, been shut away from the sound of waves and timber, and cordage. Her wings tensed, she wanted to fly up with a scream.

She walked.

They opened a door for her; she went through, and it closed behind her with sound-deadening massiveness. She saw a small, richly furred and carpeted room, where many lamps burned. The air was so thick it made her dizzy. T'heonax lay on a couch watching her, playing with one of the Eart'ho knives. There was no one else.

"Sit down," he said.

She squatted on her tail, eyes smoldering into his as if they were equals.

"What did you wish to say?" he asked tonelessly.

"The admiral your father lives?" she countered.

"Not for long, I fear," he said. "Aeak'ha will eat him before noon." His eyes went toward the arras, haunted. "How long the night is!"

Rodonis waited.

"Well?" he said. His head swung back, snakishly. There was a rawness in his tone. "You mentioned something about . . . another mutiny?"

Rodonis sat straight up on her haunches. Her crest

grew stiff. "Yes," she replied in a winter voice. "My husband's crew have not forgotten him."

"Perhaps not," snapped T'heonax. "But they've had sufficient loyalty to the Admiralty drubbed into them by now."

"Loyalty to Admiral Syranax, yes," she told him. "But that was never lacking. You know as well as I, what happened was no mutiny . . . only a riot, by males who were against you. Syranax they have always admired, if not loved.

"The *real* mutiny will be against his murderer."

T'heonax leaped.

"What do you mean?" he shouted. "Who's a murderer?"

"You are." Rodonis pushed it out between her teeth. "You have poisoned your father."

She waited then, through a time which stretched close to breaking. She could not tell if the notoriously violent male she faced would kill her for uttering those words.

Almost, he did. He drew back from her when his knife touched her throat. His jaws clashed shut again, he leaped onto his couch and stood there on all fours with back arched, tail rigid and wings rising.

"Go on," he hissed. "Say your lies. I know well enough how you hate my whole family, because of that worthless husband of yours. All the Fleet knows. Do you expect them to believe your naked word?"

"I never hated your father," said Rodonis, not quite steadily; death had brushed very close. "He condemned Delp, yes. I thought he did wrongly, but he did it for the Fleet, and I . . . I am of officer kindred myself. You recall, on the day after the raid I asked him to dine with me, as a token to all that the Drak'honai must close ranks.''

"So you did," sneered T'heonax. "A pretty gesture. I remember how hotly spiced all the guests said the food was. And the little keepsake you gave him, that shining disk from the Eart'ho possessions. Touching! As if it were yours to give. Everything of theirs belongs to the Admiralty.''

"Well, the fat Eart'ho had given it to me himself," said Rodonis. She was deliberately leading the conversation into irrelevant channels, seeking to calm them both. "He had recovered it from his baggage, he said. He called it a *coin* . . . an article of trade among his people . . . thought I might like it to remember him by. That was just after the . . . the riot . . . and just before he and his companions were removed from the *Gerunis* to that other raft.''

"It was a miser's gift," said T'heonax. "The disk was quite worn out of shape— Bah!" His muscles bunched again. "Come. Accuse me further, if you dare.''

"I have not been altogether a fool," said Rodonis. "I have left letters, to be opened by certain friends if I do not return. But consider the facts, T'heonax. You are an ambitious male, and one of whom most persons are willing to think the worst. Your father's death will make you Admiral, the virtual owner of the Fleet—how long you must have chafed, waiting for this! Your father is dying, stricken by a malady unlike any known to our chirurgeons: not even like any known poison, so wildly does it destroy him. Now it is known to many that the raiders did not manage to carry off every bit of the Eart'ho food: three small packets were left behind. The Eart'honai frequently and publicly warned us against eating any of their rations. And *you* have had charge of all the Eart'ho things!''

T'heonax gasped.

''It's a lie!'' he chattered. ''I don't know . . . I haven't . . . I never—Will anyone believe I, anyone, could do such a thing . . . poison . . . to his own father?''

''Of you they will believe it,'' said Rodonis.

''I swear by the Lodestar—!''

''The Lodestar will not give luck to a Fleet commanded by a parricide. There will be mutiny on that account alone, T'heonax.''

He glared at her, wild and panting. ''What do you want?'' he croaked.

Rodonis looked at him with the coldest gaze he had ever met. ''I will burn those letters,'' she said, ''and will keep silence forever. I will even join my denials to yours, should the same thoughts occur to someone else. But Delp must have immediate, total amnesty.''

T'heonax bristled and snarled at her.

''I could fight you,'' he growled. ''I could have you arrested for treasonable talk, and kill anyone who dared—''

"Perhaps," said Rodonis. "But is it worth it? You might split the Fleet open and leave us all a prey to the Lannach'honai. All I ask is my husband back."

"For that' you would threaten to ruin the Fleet?"

"Yes," she said.

And after a moment: "You do not understand. You males make the nations and wars and songs and science, all the little things. You imagine you are the strong, practical sex. But a female goes again and yet again under death's shadow, to bring forth another life. We are the hard ones. We have to be."

T'heonax huddled back, shivering.

"Yes," he whispered at last, "yes, curse you, shrivel you, yes, you' can have him. I'll give you an order now, this instant. Get his rotten feet off my raft before dawn, d'you hear? But I did not poison my father." His wings beat thunderous, until he lifted up under the ceiling and threshed there, trapped and screaming. "I *didn't!*"

Rodonis waited.

Presently she took the written order, and left him, and went to the brig, where they cut the ropes that bound Delp hyr Orikan. He lay in her arms and sobbed. "I will keep my wings, I will keep my wings—"

Rodonis sa Axollon stroked his crest, murmured to him, crooned to him, told him all would be well now, they were going home again, and wept a little because she loved him.

Inwardly she held a chill memory, how old Van Rijn had given her the coin but warned her against . . . what had he said? . . . heavy metal poisoning. "To you, iron, copper, tin is unknown stuffs. I am not a chemist, me; chemists I hire when chemicking is needful; but I think better I eat a shovelful arsenic than one of your cubs try teething on this piece money, by damn!''

And she remembered sitting up in the dark, with a stone in her hand, grinding and grinding the coin, until there was seasoning for the unbendable admiral's dinner.

Afterward she recollected that the Eart'ho was not supposed to have such mastery of her language. It occurred to her now, like a shudder, that he could very well have left that deadly food behind on purpose, in hopes it might cause trouble. But how closely had he foreseen the event?

XI

Guntra of the Enklann sept came in through the door. Eric Wace looked wearily up. Behind him, hugely shadowed between rush lights, the mill was a mumble of toiling forms.

"Yes?" he sighed.

Guntra held out a broad shield, two meters long, a light sturdy construction of wicker on a wooden frame. For many ten-days she had supervised hundreds of females and cubs as they gathered and split and dried the reeds, formed the wood, wove the fabric, assembled the unit. She had not been so tired since homecoming. Nevertheless, a small victory dwelt in her voice: "This is the four thousandth, Councilor." It was not his title, but the Lannacha mind could hardly imagine anyone without definite rank inside the Flock organization. Considering the authority granted the wingless creatures, it fell most naturally to call them Councilors.

"Good." He hefted the object in hands grown calloused. "A strong piece of work. Four thousand are more than enough; your task is done, Guntra."

"Thank you." She looked curiously about the transformed mill. Hard to remember that not so long ago it had existed chiefly to grind food.

Angrek of the Trekkans came up with a block of wood in his grasp. "Councilor," he began, "I—" He stopped. His gaze had fallen on Guntra, who was still in her early middle years and had always been considered handsome.

Her eyes met his. A common smokiness lit them. His wings spread and he took a stiff step toward her.

With a gasp, almost a sob, Guntra turned and fled. Angrek stared after her, then threw his block to the floor and cursed.

"What the devil?" said Wace.

Angrek beat a fist into his palm. "Ghosts," he muttered. "It must be ghosts . . . unrestful spirits of all the evildoers who ever lived . . . possessing the Drakska, and now come to plague us!"

Another pair of bodies darkened the door, which stood open to the short pale night of early summer. Nicholas van Rijn and Tolk the Herald entered.

"How goes it, boy?" boomed Van Rijn. He was gnawing a nitro-packed onion; the gauntness which had settled on Wace, even on Sandra, had not touched him. But then, thought Wace bitterly, the old blubberbucket didn't work. All he did was stroll around and talk to the local bosses and complain that things weren't proceeding fast enough.

"Slowly, sir." The younger man bit back words he would rather have said. *You bloated leech, do you expect to be carried home by my labor and my brains, and fob me off with another factor's post on another hell-planet?*

"It will have to be speeded, then," said Van Rijn. "We cannot wait so long, you and me."

Tolk glanced keenly at Angrek. The handicrafter was still trembling and whispering charms. "What's wrong?" he asked.

"The . . . an influence." Angrek covered his eyes. "Herald," he stammered, "Guntra of the Enklann was here just now, and for a moment we . . . we desired each other."

Tolk looked grave, but spoke without reproof. "It has happened to many. Keep it under control."

"But what *is* it, Herald? A sickness? A judgment? What have I done?"

"These unnatural impulses aren't unknown," said Tolk. "They crop up in most of us, every once in a while. But of course, one doesn't talk about it; one supresses it, and does his or her best to forget it ever happened." He scowled. "Lately there has been more of such hankering than usual. I don't know why. Go back to your work and avoid females."

Angrek drew a shaky breath, picked up his piece of wood, and nudged Wace. "I wanted your advice; the shape here doesn't seem to me the best for its purpose—"

Tolk looked around. He had just come back from a

prolonged journey, cruising over his entire homeland to bear word to scattered clans. "There has been much work done here," he said.

"Ja" nodded Van Rijn complacently. "He is a talented engineer, him my young friend. But then, the factor on a new planet had pestbedamned better be a good engineer."

"I am not so well acquainted with the details of his schemes."

"My schemes," corrected Van Rijn, somewhat huffily. "I tell him to make us weapons. All he does then is make them."

"All?" asked Tolk dryly. He inspected a skeletal framework. "What's this?"

"A repeating dart-thrower; a machine gun, I call it. See, this walking beam turns this spurred fly wheel. Darts are fed to the wheel on a belt—s-s-so—and tossed off fast: two or three in an eye-wink, at least. The wheel is swivel-mounted to point in all directions. It is an old idea, really, I think Miller or de Camp or someone first built it long ago. But it is one hard damn thing to face in battle."

"Excellent," approved Tolk. "And that over there?"

"We call it a ballista. It is like the Drak'ho catapults, only more so. This throws large stones, to break down a wall or sink a boat. And here—*ja*." Van Rijn picked up the shield Guntra had brought. "This is not so good advertising copy, maybe, but I think it means a bit more for us than the other machineries. A warrior on the ground wears one on his back."

"Mm-m-m . . .yes, I see where a harness would fit

it would stop missiles from above, eh? But our warrior could not fly while he wore it.''

"Just so!'' roared Van Rijn. "Just bloody-be-so! That is the troubles with you folk on Diomedes. Great balls of cheese! How you expect to fight a real war with nothing but all air forces, ha! Up here in Salmenbrok, I spend all days hammering into stupid officer heads, it is infantry takes and holds a position, by damn! And then officers have to beat it into the ranks, and practice them—gout of Judas! It is not time enough! In these few ten-days, I have to try make what needs years!''

Tolk nodded, almost casually. Even Trolwen had needed time and argument before he grasped the idea of a combat force whose main body was deliberately restricted to ground operations. It was too alien a concept. But the Herald said only: "Yes. I see your reasoning. It is the strong points which decide who holds Lannach, the fortified towns that dominate a countryside from which all the food comes. And to take the towns back, we will need to dig our way in.''

"You think smartly,'' approved Van Rijn. "In Earth history, it took some peoples a long time to learn there is no victory in air power alone.''

"There are still the Drakska fire weapons,'' said Tolk. "What do you plan to do about them? My whole mission, these past ten-days, has been largely to persuade the outlying septs to join us. I gave them your word that the fire could be faced, that we'd even have flame-throwers and bombs of our own. I'd better have been telling the truth.''

He looked about. The mill, converted to a crude

factory, was too full of winged laborers for him to see far. Nearby, a primitive lathe, somewhat improved by Wace, was turning out spearshafts and tomahawk handles. Another engine, a whirling grindstone, was new to him: it shaped ax heads and similar parts, not as good as the handmade type but formed in wholesale lots. A drop hammer knocked off flint and obsidian flakes for cutting edges; a circular saw cut wooden members; a rope-twisting machine spun faster than the eye could follow. All of it was belt-powered from the great millwheels—all of it ludicrously haywired and cranky—but it spat forth the stuff of war faster than Lannach could use, filled whole bins with surplus armament.

"It is remarkable," said Tolk. "It frightens me a little."

"I make a new way of life here," said Van Rijn expansively. "It is not this machine or that one which has already changed your history beyond changing back. It is the basic idea I have introduced: mass production."

"But the fire—"

"Wace has also begun to make us fire weapons. Sulfur they have gathered from Mount Oborch, and there are oil pools from which we are getting nice arsonish liquids. Distillation, that is another art the Drak'ho have had and you have not. Now we will have some Molotov cocktails for our own selves."

The human scowled. "But there is one thing true, my friend. We have not time to train your warriors like they should be to use this material. Soon I starve; soon your females get heavy and food must be stored." He heaved a pathetic sigh. "Though I am long dead before you folks have real sufferings."

"Not so," said Tolk grimly. "We have almost half a year left before Birthtime, true. But already we are weakened by hunger, cold, and despair. Already we have failed to perform many ceremonies—"

"Blast your ceremonies!" snapped Van Rijn. "I say it is Ulwen town we should take first, where it sits so nice overlooking Duna Brae that all the hornbeasts live at. If we have Ulwen, you have eats enough, also a strong point easy to defend. But no, Trolwen and the Council say we must strike straight for Mannenach, leaving Ulwen enemy-held in our rear, and going down clear to Sanga Bay where their rafts can get at us. For why? So you can hold some blue-befungused rite there!"

"You cannot understand," said Tolk gently. "We are too different. Even I, whose life's work it has been to deal with alien peoples, cannot grasp your attitude. But our life is the cycle of the year. It is not that we take the old gods so seriously any more—but their rituals, the rightness and decency of it all, the *belonging*—" He looked upward, into the shadow-hidden roof, where the wind hooted and rushed about the busy millwheels. "No, I don't believe that ancestral ghosts fly out there of nights. But I do believe that when I welcome High Summer back at the great rite in Mannenach, as all my forebears have done for as long as there has been a Flock . . . then I am keeping the Flock itself alive."

"Bah!" Van Rijn extended a dirt-encrusted hand to

scratch the matted beard which was engulfing his face. He couldn't shave or wash: even given anti-allergen shots, human skin wouldn't tolerate Diomedean soap. "I tell you shy you have all this ritual. First, you are a slave to the seasons, more even than any farmer on Earth back in our old days. Second, you must fly so much, and leave your homes empty all the dark time up here, that ritual is your most precious possession. It is the only thing you have not weighing too much to be carried with you everywhere."

"That's as may be," said Tolk. "The fact remains. If there is any chance of greeting the Full Day from Mannenach Standing Stones, we shall take it. The extra lives which are lost because this may not be the soundest strategy, will be offered in gladness."

"If it does not cost us the whole befouled war." Van Rijn snorted. "Devils and dandruff! My own chaplain at home, that pickle face, is not so fussy about what is proper. Why, that poor young fellow there was near making suicide now, just because he got a little bit excited over a wench out of wenching season, *nie?*"

"It isn't done," said Tolk stiffly. He walked from the shop. After a moment, Van Rijn followed.

Wace settled the point of discussion with Angrek, checked operations elsewhere, swore at a well-meaning young porter who was storing volatile petroleum fractions beside the hearth, and left. His feet were heavy at the end of his legs. It was too much for one man to do, organizing, designing, supervising, trouble-shooting— Van Rijn seemed to think it was routine to lift neolithic hunters into the machine age in a few weeks. He ought to try it himself! It might sweat some of the lard off the old hog.

The nights were so short now, only a paleness between two red clouds on a jagged horizon, that Wace no longer paid any heed to the time. He worked until he was ready to drop, slept a while, and went back to work.

Sometimes he wondered if he had ever felt rested and clean, and well fed, and comforted in his aloneness.

Morning smoldered on northerly ridges, where a line of volcanoes smeared wrathful black across the sun. Both moons were sinking, each a cold coppery disk twice the apparent size of Earth's Luna. Mount Oborch shivered along giant flanks and spat a few boulders at the pallid sky. The wind came galing, stiff as an iron bar pressed against Wace's suddenly chilled back. Salmenbrok village huddled flinty barren under its loud quick thrust.

He had reached the ladder made for him, so he could reach the tiny loft-room he used, when Sandra Tamarin came from behind the adjoining tower. She paused, one hand stealing to her face. He could not hear what she said, in the blustery air.

He went over to her. Gravel scrunched under the awkward leather boots a Lannacha tailor had made him. "I beg your pardon, my lady?"

"Oh . . . it was nothing, Freeman Wace." Her green gaze came up to meet his, steadily and proudly, but he saw a redness steal along her cheeks. "I only said good morning."

"Likewise." He rubbed sandy-lidded eyes. "I haven't seen you for some time, my lady. How are you?"

"Restless," she said. "Unhappy. Will you talk to me for a little, perhaps?"

They left the hamlet behind and followed a dim trail upward, through low harsh bushes breaking into purple bloom. High above them wheeled a few sentries, but those were only impersonal specks against heaven. Wace felt his heartbeat grow hasty.

"What have you been doing?" he asked.

"Nothing of value. What can I do?" She stared down at her hands. "I try, but I have not the skills, not like you the engineer or Freeman van Rijn."

"Him?" Wace shrugged. No doubt the old goat had found plenty of chance to brag himself up, as he lounged superfluous around Salmenbrok. "It—" He stopped, groping after words. "It's enough just to have my lady present."

"Why, Freeman!" She laughed, with genuine half-amused pleasure and no coyness at all. "I never thought you so gallant in the words."

"Never had much chance to be, my lady," he murmured, too tired and strength-emptied to keep up his guard.

"Not?" She gave him a sideways look. The wind laid its fingers in her tightly braided hair and unfurled small argent banners of it. She was not yet starved, but the bones in her face were standing out more sharply; there was a smudge on one cheek and her garments were clumsy baggings hurled together by a tailor who had never seen a human frame before. But somehow, stripped thus of queenliness, she seemed to him more beautiful than erstwhile—perhaps because of being closer? Because her poverty said with frankness that she was only human flesh like himself?

"No," he got out between stiff lips.

"I do not understand," she said.

"Your pardon, my lady. I was thinking out loud. Bad habit. But one does, on these outpost worlds. You see the same few men so often that they stop being company; you avoid them—and, of course, we're always undermanned, so you have to go out by yourself on various jobs, maybe for weeks at a time. Why am I saying all this? I don't know. Dear God, how tired I am!"

They paused on a ridge. At their feet there was a cliff tumbling through hundreds of meters down to a foam-white river. Across the canyon were mountains and mountains, their snows tinged bloody by the sun. The wind came streaking up the dales and struck the humans in the face.

"I see. Yes, it clears for me." Sandra regarded him with grave eyes. "You have had to work hard all your life. There has not been time for the pleasures, the learned manners and culture. Not?"

"No time at all, my lady," he said "I was born in the slums, one kilometer from the old Triton Docks. Nobody but the very poor would live that close to a spaceport, the traffic and stinks and earthquake noise . . . though you got used to it, still it was a part of you, built into your bones. Half my playmates are now

dead or in jail, I imagine, and the other half are scrab-
bling for the occasional half-skilled hard-and-dirty job
no one else wants. Don't pity me, though. I was lucky.
I got apprenticed to a fur wholesaler when I was twelve.
After two years, I'd made enough contacts to get a
hard-and-dirty job myself—only this was on a spaceship, fur-trapping expedition to Rhiannon. I taught
myself a little something in odd moments, and bluffed
about the rest I was supposed to know, and got a
slightly better job. And so on and so on, till they put me
in charge of this outpost . . . a very minor enterprise,
which may in time become moderately profitable but
will never be important. But it's a stepping stone. So
here I am, on a mountain top with all Diomedes below
me, and what's next?"

He shook his head, violently, wondering why his
reserve had broken down. Being so exhausted was like
a drunkenness. But more to it than that . . . no, he was
not fishing for sympathy. . . . down underneath, did he
want to find out if she would understand? If she could?

"You will get back," she said quietly. "Your kind
of man survives."

"Maybe!"

"It is heroic, what you have done already." She
looked away from him, toward the driving clouds
around Oborch's peak. "I am not certain anything can
stop you. Except yourself."

"I?" He was beginning to be embarrassed now, and
wanted to talk of other things. He plucked at his bristly
red beard.

"Yes. Who else can? You have come so far, so fast.

But why not stop? Soon, perhaps here on this mountain, must you not ask yourself how much farther it is worth going?"

"I don't know. As far as possible, I guess."

"Why? Is it necessary to become great? Is it not enough to be free? With your talent and experience, you can make good-enough monies on many settled planets where men are more at home than here. Like Hermes, *exemplia*. In this striving to be rich and powerful, is it not merely that you want to feed and shelter the little boy who once cried himself hungry to sleep back in Triton Docks? But that little boy you can never comfort, my friend. He died long ago."

"Well . . . I don't know . . . I suppose one day I'll have a family. I'd want to give my wife more than just a living; I'd want to leave my children and grandchildren enough resources to go on—to stand off the whole world if they have to—"

"Yes. So. I think maybe—" he saw, before she turned her head from him, how the blood flew up into her face— "the old fighting Dukes of Hermes were like so. It would be well if we had a breed of men like them again—" Suddenly she began walking very fast down the path. "Enough. Best we return, not?"

He followed her, little aware of the ground he trod.

XII

When the Lannachska were ready to fight, they were called to Salmenbrok by Tolk's Whistlers until the sky darkened with their wings. Then Trolwen made his way through a seethe of warriors to Van Rijn.

"Surely the gods are weary of us," he said bitterly. "Near always, at this time of year, there are strong south winds." He gestured at a breathless heaven. "Do you know a spell for raising dead breezes?"

The merchant looked up, somewhat annoyed. He was seated at a table outside the wattle-and-clay hut they had built for him beyond the village—for he refused to climb ladders, or sleep in a damp cave—dicing with Corps Captain Srygen for the beryl-like gemstones which were a local medium of exchange. The number of species in the galaxy which have independently invented some form of African golf is beyond estimation.

"Well," he snapped, "and why must you have your tail fanned? . . . Ah, seven! No, pox and pills, I remember, here seven is not a so good number. Well, we try again." The three cubes clicked in his hand and across the table. "Hm-m-m, seven again." He scooped up the stakes. "Double or nothings?"

"The ghost-eaters take it!" Srygen got up. "You've been winning too motherless often for my taste."

Van Rijn surged to his own feet like a broaching whale. "By damn, you take that back or—"

"I said nothing challengeable," Srygen told him coldly.

"You implied it. I am insulted, myself!"

"Hold on there," growled Trolwen. "What do you think this is, a beer feast? Eart'a, all the fighting forces of Lannach are now gathered on these hills. We cannot feed them here very long. And yet, with the new weapons loaded on the railway cars, we cannot stir until there is a south wind. What to do?"

Van Rijn glared at Srygen. "I said I was insulted. I do not think so good when I am insulted."

"I am sure the captain will apologize for any unintended offense," said Trolwen, with a red-shot look at them both.

"Indeed," said Srygen. He spoke it like pulling teeth.

"So." Van Rijn stroked his beard. "Then to prove you make no doubt about my honesties, we throw once more, *nie?* Double or nothings."

Srygen snatched the dice and hurled them. "Ah, a six you have," said Van Rijn. "It is not so easy to beat. I am afraid I have already lost. It is not so simple to be a poor tired hungry old man, far away from his home and from the Siamese cats who are all he has to love him for himself, not just his monies. . . . Tum-te-tum-te-tum. . . . Eight! A two, a three, a three! Well, well, well!"

"Transport," said Trolwen, hanging on to his temper by a hair. "The new weapons are too heavy for our porters. They have to go by rail. Without a wind, how do we get them down to Sagna Bay?"

"Simple," said Van Rijn, counting his take. "Till you get a good wind, tie ropes to the cars and all these so-husky young fellows pull."

Srygen blew up. "A free clan male, to drag a car like a . . . like a *Draka?*" He mastered himself and choked: "It isn't done."

"Sometimes," said Van Rijn, "these things must be done." He scooped up the jewels, dropped them into a purse, and went over to a well. "Surely you have some disciplines in this Flock."

"Oh . . . yes . . . I suppose so—" Trolwen's unhappy gaze went down-slope to the brawling, shouting winged tide which had engulfed the village. "But sustained labor like that has always . . . long before the Drakska came . . . always been considered—perverted, in a way—it is not exactly forbidden, but one does not do it without the most compelling necessity. To labor in *public*—No!"

Van Rijn hauled on the windlass. "Why not? The

Drak'honai, them, make all kinds tiresome preach-
ments about the dignity of labor. For them it is needful;
in their way of life, one must work hard. But for you?
Why must one *not* work hard in Lannach?''

''It isn't right,'' said Srygen stiffly. ''It makes us
like some kind of animal.''

Van Rijn pulled the bucket to the well coping and
took a bottle of Earthside beer from it. ''Ahhh, good
and cold . . . hm-m-m, possibly too cold, damn all
places without thermostatted coolers—'' He opened
the bottle on the stone curb and tasted. ''It will do.
Now, I have made travels, and I find that everywhere
the manners and morals of peoples have some good
reason at bottom. Maybe the race has forgotten why
was a rule made in the first place, but if the rule does not
make some sense, it will not last many centuries. Fol-
lows then that you do not like prolonged hard work,
except to be sure migration, because it is not good for
you for some reason. And yet it does not hurt the
Drak'honai too much. Paradox!''

''Unlawfulness take your wonderings,'' snarled
Trolwen. ''It was your idea that we make all this
new-fangled apparatus, instead of fighting as our males
have always fought. Now, how do we get it down to the
lowlands without demoralizing the army?''

''Oh, that!'' Van Rijn shrugged. ''You have
sports—contests—*nie?*''

''Of course.''

''Well, you explain these cars must be brought with
us and, while it is not necessary we leave at once—''

''But it is! We'll starve if we don't!''

"My good young friend," said Van Rijn patiently, "I see plain you have much to learn about politics. You Lannachska do not understand lying, I suppose because you do not get married. You tell the warriors, I say, that we can wait for a south wind all right but you know they are eager to come to grips with the foe and therefore they will be invited to play a small game. Each clan will pull so and so many cars down, and we time how fast it goes and make a prize for the best pullers."

"Well, I'll be accursed," said Srygen.

Trolwen nodded eagerly. "It's just the sort of thing that gets into clan traditions—"

"You see," explained Van Rijn, "it is what we call semantics on Earth. I am old and short with breath, so I can look unprejudiced at all these footballs and baseballs and potato races, and I know that a game is hard work you are not required to do."

He belched, opened another bottle, and took a half-eaten salami from his purse. The supplies weren't going to last very much longer.

XIII

When the expedition was halfway down the Misty Mountains, their wind rose behind them. A hundred warriors harnessed to each railway car relaxed and waited for the timers whose hourglasses would determine the winning team.

"But they are not all so dim in the brain, surely," said Sandra.

"Oh, no," answered Wace. "But those who were smart enough to see through Old Nick's scheme were also smart enough to see it was necessary, and keep quiet."

He huddled in a mordant blast that drove down alpine slopes to the distant cloudy green of hills and valleys, and watched the engineers at work. A train consisted of about thirty light little cars roped together, with a "locomotive" at the head and another in the middle. These were somewhat more sturdily built, to support two high masts with square sails. Given wood of almost metallic hardness, plus an oil-drip over the wheels in lieu of ball bearings, plus the hurricane thrust of Diomedean winds, the system became practical. You didn't get up much speed, and you must often wait for a following wind, but this was not a culture bound to hourly schedules.

"It's not too late for you to go back, my lady," said Wace. "I can arrange an escort."

"No." She laid a hand on the bow which had been made for her—no toy, a 25-kilo killing tool such as she had often hunted with in her home forests. Her head lifted, the silverpale hair caught chill ruddy sunlight and threw back a glow to this dark immensity of cliffs and glaciers. "Here we all stand or we all die. It would not be right for a ruler born to stay home."

Van Rijn hawked. "Trouble with aristocrats," he muttered. "Bred for looks and courage, not brains. Now *I* would go back, if not needed here to show I have confidence in my own plans."

"Do you?" asked Wace skeptically.

"Let be with foolishness," snorted Van Rijn. "Of course not." He trudged back to the staff car which had been prepared for him: at least it had walls, a roof, and a bunk. The wind shrieked down ringing stony canyons, he leaned against it with all his weight. Overhead swooped and soared the squadrons of Lannach.

Wace and Sandra each had a private car, but she asked him to ride down with her. "Forgive me if I make dramatics, Eric, but we may be killed and it is lonely to die without a human hand to hold." She laughed, a little breathlessly. "Or at least we can talk."

"I'm afraid—" He cleared a tightened throat. "I'm afraid, my lady, I can't converse as readily as . . . Freeman Van Rijn."

"Oh," she grinned, "that was what I meant. I said *we* can talk, not him only."

Nevertheless, when the trains got into motion, she grew as quiet as he.

Lacking their watches they could scarcely even guess how long the trip took. High summer had almost come to Lannach; once in twelve and a half hours, the sun scraped the horizon north of west, but there was no more real night. Wace watched the kilometers click away beneath him; he ate, slept, spoke desultorily with Sandra or with young Angrek who served as her aide, and the great land flattened into rolling valleys and forests of low fringe-leaved trees, and the sea came near.

Now and again a hotbox or a contrary wind delayed the caravan. There was restlessness in the ranks: they were used to streaking in a day from the mountains to the coast, not to wheeling above this inchworm or a railway. Drak'honai scouts spied them from afar, inevitably, and a detachment of rafts lumbered into Sagna Bay with powerful reinforcements. Raids probed the flanks of the attackers. And still the trains must crawl.

In point of fact, there were eight Diomedean revolutions between the departure from Salmenbrok and the Battle of Mannenach.

The harbor town lay on the Sagna shore, well in from the open sea and sheltered by surrounding wooded hills. It was a gaunt grim-looking complex of stone towers, tightly knitted together with the usual tunnels and enclosed bridges, talking in the harsh tones of half a dozen big windmills. It overlooked a small pier, which the Drak'honai had been enlarging. Beyond, dark on the choppy brown waters, rocked two score enemy craft.

As his train halted, Wace jumped from Sandra's car. There was nothing to shoot at yet: Mannenach revealed only a few peaked roofs thrusting above the grassy ridge before him. Even against the wind, he could hear the thunder of wings as the Drak'honai lifted from the town, twisting upward in a single black mass like some tornado made flesh. But heaven was thick with Lannachska above him, and the enemy made no immediate attack.

His heart thumped, runaway, and his mouth was too dry for him to speak. Almost hazily, he saw Sandra beside him. A Diomedean bodyguard under Angrek closed around in a thornbush of spears.

The girl smiled. "This is a kind of relief," she said. "No more sitting and worrying, only to do what we can, not?"

"Not indeed!" puffed Van Rijn, stumping toward them. Like the other humans, he had arranged for an ill-fitting cuirass and helmet of laminated hard leather above the baggy malodorous native clothes. But he wore two sets of armor, one on top of the other, carried a shield on his left arm, had deputed two young warriors to hold another shield over him like a canopy, and bore a tomahawk and a beltful of stone daggers. ''Not if I can get out of it, by damn! You go ahead and fight. I will be right behind you—as far behind as the good saints let.''

Wace found his tongue and said maliciously: ''I've often thought there might be fewer wars among civilized races, if they reverted to this primitive custom that the generals are present at the battles.''

''Bah! Ridiculous! Just as many wars, only using generals who have guts more than brains. I think cowards make the best strategists, stands to reason, by damn. Now I stay in my car.'' Van Rijn stalked off, muttering.

Trolwen's newly-formed field artillery corps were going frantic, unloading their clumsy weapons from the trains and assembling them while squads and patrols skirmished overhead. Wace cursed—here was something he could do!—and hurried to the nearest confusion. ''Hoy, there! Back away! What are you trying to do? Here, you, you, you, get up in the car and unlash the main frame . . . that piece *there,* you clothead!'' After a while, he almost lost consciousness of the fighting that developed around him.

The Mannenach garrison and its sea-borne reinforcements had begun with cautious probing, a few squadrons at a time swooping to flurry briefly with some of the Lannachska flying troops and then pull away again toward the town. Drak'ho forces here were outnumbered by a fair margin; Trolwen had reasoned correctly that no admiral would dare leave the main

Fleet without a strong defense while Lannach was still formidable. In addition, the sailors were puzzled, a little afraid, at the unprecedented attacking formations.

Fully half the Lannachska were ranked on the ground, covered by rooflike shields which would not even permit them to fly! Never in history had such a thing been known!

During an hour, the two hordes came more closely to grips. Much superior in the air, the Drak'honai punched time after time through Trolwen's fliers. But integrated by the Whistler corps, the aerial troops closed again, fluidly. And there was little profit in attacking the Lannachska infantry—those awkward wicker shields trapped edged missiles, sent stones rebounding, an assault from above was almost ignored.

Arrows were falling thickly when Wace had his last fieldpiece assembled. He nodded at a Whistler, who whirled up immediately to bear the word to Trolwen. From the commander's position, where he rode a thermal updraft, came a burst of messengers—banners broke out on the ground, war whoops tore through the wind, it was the word to advance!

Ringed by Angrek's guards, Wace remained all too well aware that he was at the forefront of an army. Sandra went beside him, her lips untense. On either hand stretched spear-jagged lines of walking dragons. It seemed like a long time before they had mounted the ridge.

One by one, Drak'honai officers realized . . . and yelled their bafflement.

These stolid ground troops, unassailable from

above, unopposed below, were simply pouring over the hill to Mannenach's walls, trundling their siege tools. When they arrived there, they got to work.

It became a gale of wings and weapons. The Drak'honai plunged, hacked and stabbed at Trolwen's infantry—and were in their turn attacked from above, as his fliers whom they had briefly dispersed resumed formation. Meanwhile, *crunch, crunch, crunch,* rams ate at Mannenach; detachments on foot went around the town and down toward the harbor.

"Over there! Hit 'em again!" Wace heard all at once that he was yelling.

Something broke through the chaos overhead. An arrow-filled body crashed to earth. A live one followed it, a Drak'ho warrior with the air pistol-cracking under his wings. He came low and fast; one of Angrek's lads thrust a sword at him, missed, and had his brains spattered by the sailor's tomahawk.

Without time to know what had happened, Wace saw the creature before him. He struck, wildly, with his own stone ax. A wing-buffet knocked him to the ground. He bounced up, spitting blood, as the Drak'ho came about and dove again. His hands were empty— Suddenly the Drak'ho screamed and clawed at an arrow in his throat, fluttered down and died.

Sandra nocked a fresh shaft. "I told you I would have some small use today," she said.

"I—" Wace reeled where he stood, looking at her.

"Go on," she said. "Help them break through. I will guard."

Her face was even paler than before, but there was a green in her eyes which burned.

He spun about and went back to directing his sappers. It was plain now that battering rams had been a mistake; they wouldn't get through mortared walls till Matthewsmas. He took everyone off the engines and put them to helping those who dug. With enough wooden shovels—or bare hands—they'd be sure to strike a tunnel soon.

From somewhere near, there lifted a clatter great enough to drown out the struggle around him. Wace jumped up on a ram's framework and looked over the heads of his engineers.

A body of Drak'honai had resorted to the ground themselves. They were not drilled in such tactics; but then, the Lannachska had had only the sketchiest training. By sheer sustained fury the Drak'honai were pushing their opponents back. From Trolwen's airy viewpoint, thought Wace, there must be an ugly dent in the line.

Where the devil were the machine guns?

Yes, here came one, bouncing along on a little cart. Two Lannachska began pumping the flywheel, a third aimed and operated the feed. Darts hosed across the Drak'honai. They broke up, took to the sky again. Wace hugged Sandra and danced her across the field.

Then hell boiled over on the roofs above him. His immediate corps had finally gotten to an underground passage and made it a way of entry. Driving the enemy before them, up to the top floors and out, they seized this one tower in a rush.

"Angrek!" panted Wace. "Get me up there!" Someone lowered a rope. He swarmed up it, with Sandra close behind. Standing on the ridgepole, he looked past stony parapets and turning millwheels, down to the bay. Trolwen's forces had taken the pier without much trouble. But they were getting no farther: a steady hair of fire-streams, oil bombs, and catapult missiles from the anchored rafts staved them off. Their own similar armament was outranged.

Sandra squinted against the wind, shifted north to lash her eyes to weeping, and pointed "Eric—do you recognize that flag, on the largest of the vessels there?"

"Hm-m-m . . . let me see . . . yes, I do. Isn't that our old chum Delp's personal banner?"

"So, it is. I am not sorry he has escaped punishment for the riot we made. But I would rather have someone else to fight, it would be safer."

"Maybe," said Wace. "But there's work to do. We have our toe hold in the city. Now we'll have to beat down doors and push out the enemy—room by room—and you're staying here!"

"I am not!"

Wace jerked his thumb at Angrek. "Detail a squad to take the lady back to the trains," he snapped.

"No!" yelled Sandra.

"You're too late," grinned Wace. "I arranged for this before we ever left Salmenbrok."

She swore at him—then suddenly, softly, she leaned over and murmured beneath the wind and the war-shrieks: "Come back hale, my friend."

He led his troopers into the tower.

Afterward he had no clear memory of the fight. It was a hard and bloody operation, ax and knife, tooth and fist, wing and tail, in narrow tunnels and cavelike rooms. He took blows, and gave them; once, for several minutes, he lay unconscious, and once he led a triumphant breakthrough into a wide assembly hall. He was not fanged, winged, or caudate himself, but he was heavier than any Diomedean, his blows seldom had to be repeated.

The Lannachska took Mannenach because they had—not training enough to make them good ground fighters—but enough to give them the *concept* of battle with immobilized wings. It was as revolting to Diomedean instincts as the idea of fighting with teeth alone, hands bound, would be to a human; unprepared for it, the Drak'honai bolted and ran ratlike down the tunnels in search of open sky.

Hours afterward, staggering with exhaustion, Wace climbed to a flat roof at the other end of town. Tolk sat there waiting for him.

"I think . . . we have . . . it all now," gasped the human.

"And yet not enough," said Tolk haggardly. "Look at the bay."

Wace grabbed the parapet to steady himself.

There was no more pier, no more sheds at the waterfront—it all stood in one black smoke. But the rafts and canoes of Drak'ho had edged into the shallows, forming a bridge to shore; and over this the sailors were dragging dismounted catapults and flamethrowers.

"They have too good a commander," said Tolk. "He has gotten the idea too fast, that our new methods have their own weaknesses."

"What is . . . Delp . . . going to do?" whispered Wace.

"Stay and see," suggested the Herald. "There is no way for us to help."

The Drak'honai were still superior in the air. Looking up toward a sky low and gloomy, rain clouds driving across angry gunmetal waters. Wace saw them moving to envelope the Lannacha air cover.

"You see," said Tolk, "it is true that their fliers cannot do much against our walkers—but the enemy chief has realized that the converse is also true."

Trolwen was too good a tactician himself to be cut up in such a fashion. Fighting every centimeter, his fliers retreated. After a while there was nothing in the sky but gray wrack.

Down on the ground, covered by arcing bombardment from the rafts, the sailors were setting up their mobile artillery. They had more of it than the Lannachska, and were better shots. A few infantry charges broke up in bloody ruin.

"Our machine guns they do not possess, of course," said Tolk. "But then, we do not have enough to make the difference."

Wace whirled on Angrek, who had joined him. "Don't stand here!" he cried. "Let's get down—rally our folk—seize those— It can be done, I tell you!"

"Theoretically, yes." Tolk nodded his lean head. "I can see where a person on the ground, taking advantage of every bit of cover, might squirm his way up to those catapults and flamethrowers, and tomahawk the operators. But in practice—well, we do not have such skill."

"Then what would you do?" groaned Wace.

"Let us first consider what will assuredly happen," said Tolk. "We have lost our trains; if not captured, they will be fired presently. Thus our supplies are gone. Our forces have been split, the fliers driven off, we groundlings left here. Trolwen cannot fight his way back to us, being outnumbered. We at Mannenach do outnumber our immediate opponents by quite a bit. But we cannot face their artillery.

"Therefore, to continue the fight, we must throw away all our big shields and other new-gangled items, and revert to conventional air tactics. But this infantry is not well equipped for normal combat: we have few archers, for instance. Delp need only shelter on the rafts, behind his fire weapons, and for all our greater numbers we'll be unable to touch him. Meanwhile he will have us pinned here, cut off from food and material. All the excess war goods your mill produced is valueless lying up in Salmenbrok. And there will certainly be strong reinforcements from the Fleet."

"To hell with that!" shouted Wace. "We have the town, don't we? We can hold it against them till they rot!"

"What can we eat while they are rotting?" said Tolk. "You are a good craftsman, Eart'a, but no student of war. The cold fact is, that Delp managed to split our forces, and therefore he has already won. I propose to cut our losses by retreating now, while we still can."

And then suddenly his manner broke, and he stooped and covered his eyes with his wings. Wace saw that the Herald was growing old.

XIV

There was dancing on the decks, and jubilant chants rang across Sagna Bay to the enfolding hills. Up and down and around, in and out, the feet and the wings interwove till timbers trembled. High in the rigging, a piper skirled their melody; down below, a great overseer's drum which set the pace of the oars now thuttered their stamping rhythm. In a ring of wing-folded bodies, sweat-gleaming fur and eyes aglisten, a sailor whirled his female while a hundred deep voices roared the song:

". . . A-sailing, a sailing,
a-sailing to the Sea of Beer,
fair lady, spread your sun-bright
    wings
and sail with me!"

Delp walked out on the poop and looked down at his folk.

"There'll be many a new soul in the Fleet, sixty ten-days hence," he laughed.

Rodonis held his hand, tightly. "I wish—" she began.

"Yes?"

"Sometimes . . . oh, it's nothing—" The dancing pair fluttered upward, and another couple sprang out to beat the deck in their place; planks groaned under one more huge ale barrel, rolled forth to celebrate victory. "Sometimes I wish we could be like them."

"And live in the forecastle?" said Delp dryly.

"Well, no . . . of course not—"

"There's a price on the apartment, and the servants, and the bright clothes and leisure," said Delp. His eyes grew pale. "I'm about to pay some more of it."

His tail stroked briefly over her back, then he beat wings and lifted into the air. A dozen armed males followed him. So did the eyes of Rodonis.

Under Mannenach's battered walls the Drak'ho rafts lay crowded, the disorder of war not yet cleaned up in the haste to enjoy a hard-bought victory. Only the full-time warriors remained alert, though no one else would need much warning if there should be an attack. It was the boast of the forecastle that a Fleet sailor, drunk and with a female on his knee, could outfight any three foreigners sober.

Delp, flapping across calm waters under a high cloudless day-sky, found himself weighing the morale value of such a pride against the sharp practical fact that a Lannach'ho fought like ten devils. The Drak'honai had won *this* time.

A cluster of swift canoes floated aloof, the admiral's standard drooping from one garlanded masthead. T'heonax had come at Delp's urgent request, instead of making him go out to the main Fleet—which might mean that T'heonax was prepared to bury the old hatred. (Rodonis would tell her husband nothing of what had passed between them, and he did not urge her; but it was perfectly obvious she had forced the pardon from the heir in some way.) Far more likely, though, the new admiral had come to keep an eye on this untrusted captain, who had so upset things by turning the holding operation on which he had been contemptuously ordered, into a major victory. It was not unknown for a field commander with such prestige to hoist the rebel flag and try for the Admiralty.

Delp, who had no respect for T'heonax but positive reverence for the office, bitterly resented that imputation.

He landed on the outrigger as prescribed and waited until the Horn of Welcome was blown on board. It took longer than necessary. Swallowing anger, Delp flapped to the canoe and prostrated himself.

"Rise," said T'heonax in an indifferent tone. "Congratulations on your success. Now, you wished to confer with me?" He patted down a yawn. "Please do."

Delp looked around at the faces of officers, warriors, and crewfolk. "In private, with the admiral's most trusted advisors, if it please him," he said.

"Oh? Do you consider what you have to say is that important?" T'heonax nudged a young aristocrat beside him and winked.

Delp spread his wings, remembered where he was, and nodded. His neck was so stiff it hurt. "Yes, sir, I do," he got out.

"Very well." T'heonax walked leisurely toward his cabin.

It was large enough for four, but only the two of them entered, with the young court favorite, who lay down and closed his eyes in boredom. "Does not the admiral wish advice?" asked Delp.

T'heonax smiled. "So you don't intend to give me advice yourself, captain?"

Delp counted mentally to twenty, unclenched his teeth, and said:

"As the admiral wishes. I've been thinking about our basic strategy, and the battle here has rather alarmed me—"

"I didn't know you were frightened."

"Admiral, I . . . never mind! Look here sir, the enemy came within two fishhooks of beating us. They had the town. We've captured weapons from them equal or superior to our own, including a few gadgets I've never seen or heard of . . . and in incredible quantities, considering how little time they had to manufacture the stuff. Then too, they had these abominable new tactics, ground fighting—not as an incidental, like when we board an enemy raft, but as the main part of their effort!

"The only reason they lost was insufficient coordination between ground and air, and insufficient flexibility. They should have been ready to toss away their shields and take to the air in fully equipped squadrons at an instant's notice.

"And I don't think they'll neglect to remedy that fault, if we give them the chance."

T'heonax buffed his nails on a sleek-furred arm and regarded them critically. "I don't like defeatists," he said.

"Admiral, I'm just trying not to underestimate them. It's pretty clear they got all these new ideas from the Eart'honai. What else do the Eart'honai know?"

"Hm-m-m. Yes." T'heonax raised his head. A moment's uneasiness flickered in his gaze. "True. What do you propose?"

"They're off balance now," said Delp with rising eagerness. "I'm sure the disappointment has demoralized them. And of course, they've lost all that heavy equipment. If we hit them hard, we can end the war. What we must do is inflict a decisive defeat on their entire army. Then they'll have to give up, yield this country to us or die like insects when their birthing time comes."

"Yes." T'heonax smiled in a pleased way. "Like insects. Like dirty, filthy insects. We won't let them emigrate, captain."

"They deserve their chance," protested Delp.

"That's a question of high policy, captain, for me to decide."

"I'm . . . sorry, sir." After a moment: "But will the admiral, then, assign the bulk of our fighting forces to . . . to some reliable officer, with orders to hunt out the Lannach'honai?"

"You don't know just where they are?"

"They could be almost anywhere in the uplands, sir. That is, we have prisoners who can be made to guide us and give some information; Intelligence says their headquarters is a place called, Psalmenbrox. But of course they can melt into the lands." Delp shuddered. To him, whose world had been lonely islands and flat sea horizon, there was horror in the tilted mountains. "It has infinite cover to hide them. This will be no easy campaign."

"How do you propose to wage it all?" asked T'heonax querulously. He did not like to be reminded, on top of a victory celebration and a good dinner, that there was still much death ahead of him.

"By forcing them to meet us in an all-out encounter, sir. I want to take our main fighting strength, and some native guides compelled to help us, and go from town to town up there, systematically razing whatever we find, burning the woods and slaughtering the game. Give them no chance for the large battues on which they must depend to feed their females and cubs. Sooner or later, and probably sooner, they will have to gather every male and meet us. That's when I'll break them."

"I see." T'heonax nodded. Then, with a grin: "And if they break you?"

"They won't."

"It is written: 'The Lodestar shines for no single nation.' "

"The admiral knows there's always some risk in

war. But I'm convinced there's less danger in my plan than in hanging about down here, waiting for the Eart'honai to perfect some new devilment."

T'heonax's forefinger stabbed at Delp. "Ah-hah! Have you forgotten' their food will soon be all gone? We can count them out."

"I wonder—"

"Be quiet!" shrilled T'heonax.

After a little time, he went on: "Don't forget, this enormous expeditionary force of yours would leave the Fleet ill defended. And without the Fleet, the rafts, we ourselves are finished."

"Oh, don't be afraid of attack, sir—" began Delp in an eager voice.

"Afraid!" T'heonax puffed himself out. "Captain, it is treason to hint that the admiral is a . . . is not fully competent."

"I didn't mean—"

"I shall not press the matter," said T'heonax smoothly. "However, you may either make full abasement, craving my pardon, or leave my presence."

Delp stood up. His lips peeled back from the fangs, all the race memory of animal forebears who had been hunters bade him tear out the other's throat. T'heonax crouched, ready to scream for help.

Very slowly, Delp mastered himself. He half turned to go. He paused, fists jammed into balls and the membrane of his wings swollen with blood.

"Well?" smiled T'heonax.

Like an ill-designed machine, Delp went down on

his belly. "I abase myself," he mumbled. "I eat your offal. I declare that my fathers were the slaves of your fathers. Like a netted fish, I gasp for pardon."

T'heonax enjoyed himself. The fact that Delp had been so cleverly trapped between his pride and his wish to serve the Fleet, made it all the sweeter.

"Very good, captain," said the admiral when the ceremony was done. "Be thankful I didn't make you do this publicly. Now let me hear your argument. I believe you were saying something about the protection of our rafts."

"Yes . . . yes, sir. I was saying . . . the rafts need not fear the enemy."

"Indeed? True, they lie well out at sea, but not too far to reach in a few hours. What's to prevent the Flock army from assembling, unknown to you, in the mountains, then attacking the rafts before you can come to our help?"

"I would only hope they do so, sir." Delp recovered a little enthusiasm. "But I'm afraid their leadership isn't that stupid. Since when . . . I mean . . . at no time in naval history, sir, has a flying force, unsupported from the water, been able to overcome a fleet. At best, and at heavy cost, it can capture one or two rafts . . . temporarily, as in the raid when they stole the Eart'honai. Then the other vessels move in and drive it off. You see, sir, flyers can't use the engines of war, catapults and flamethrowers and so on, which alone can reduce a naval organization. Whereas the raft crews can stand under shelters and fire upward, picking the fliers off at leisure."

"Of course." T'heonax nodded. "All this is so obvious as to be a gross waste of my time. But your idea is, I take it, that a small cadre of guards would suffice to hold off a Lannach'ho attack of any size."

"And, if we're lucky, keep the enemy busy out at sea till I could arrive with our main forces. But as I said, sir, they must have brains enough not to try it."

"You assume a great deal, captain," murmured T'heonax. "You assume, not merely that I will let you go into the mountains at all, but that I will put you in command."

Delp bent his head and drooped his wings. "Apology, sir."

"I think . . . yes, I think it would be best if you just stayed here at Mannenach with your immediate flotilla."

"As the admiral wishes. Will he consider my plan, though?"

"Aeak'ha eat you!" snarled T'heonax. "I've no love for you, Delp, as well you know; but your scheme is good, and you're the best one to carry it through. I shall appoint you in charge."

Delp stood as if struck with a maul.

"Get out," said T'heonax. "We will have an official conference later."

"I thank my lord admiral—"

"Go, I said!"

When Delp had gone, T'heonax turned to his favorite. "Don't look so worried," he said. "I know what you're thinking. The fellow will win his campaign, and become still more popular, and somewhere along the line he will get ideas about seizing the Admiralty."

"I only wondered how my lord planned to prevent that," said the courtier.

"Simple enough." T'heonax grinned. "I know his type. As long as the war goes on, there's no danger of rebellion from him. So, let him break the Lannach'honai as he wishes. He'll pursue their remnants, to make sure of finishing the job. And in that pursuit—a stray arrow from somewhere—most regrettable—these things are easy to arrange. Yes."

XV

This atmosphere carried the dust particles which are the nuclei of water condensation to a higher, hence colder altitude. Thus Diomedes had more clouds and precipitation of all kinds than Earth. On a clear night you saw fewer stars; on a foggy night you did not see at all.

Mist rolled up through stony dales, until the young High Summer became a dripping chill twilight. The hordes lairing about Salmenbrok mumbled in their hunger and hopelessness: now the sun itself had withdrawn from them.

No campfires glowed, the wood of this region had all been burned. And the hinterland had been scoured clean of game, unripe wild grains, the very worms and insects, eaten by these many warriors. Now, in an eerie dank dark, only the wind and the rushing glacial waters lived . . . and Mount Oborch, sullenly prophesying deep in the earth.

Trolwen and Tolk went from the despair of their chieftains, over narrow trails where fog smoked and the high thin houses stood unreal, to the mill where the Eart'ska worked.

Here alone, it seemed, there was existence—fires still burned, stored water came down flumes to turn the wind-abandoned wheels, movement went under flickering tapers as lathes chattered and hammers thumped. Somehow, in some impossible fashion, Nicholas van Rijn had roared down the embittered protests of Angrek's gang, and their factory was at work.

Working for what? thought Trolwen, in a mind as gray as the mist.

Van Rijn himself met them at the door. He folded massive arms on hairy breast and said: "How do you, my friends? Here it goes well, we have soon a many artillery pieces ready."

"And what use will they be?" said Trolwen. "Oh, yes, we have enough to make Salmenbrok well-nigh impregnable. Which means, we could hole up here and let the enemy ring us in till we starve."

"Speak not to me of starving." Van Rijn fished in his pouch, extracted a dry bit of cheese, and regarded it mournfully. "To think, this was not so long ago a rich delicious Swiss. Now, not to rats would I offer it." He stuffed it into his mouth and chewed noisily. "My problem of belly stoking is worse than yours. *Imprimis*, the high boiling point of water here makes this a world of very bad cooks, with no idea about controlled temperatures. *Secundus*, did your porters haul me through the air, all that long lumpy way from Mannenach, to let me hunger into death?''

"I could wish we'd left you down there!" flared Trolwen.

"No," said Tolk. "He and his friends have striven, Flockchief."

"Forgive me," said Trolwen contritely. "It was only . . . I got the news . . . the Lannachska have just destroyed Eiseldrae."

"An empty town, *nie?*"

"A holy town. And they set afire the woods around it." Trolwen arched his back. "This can't go on! Soon, even if we should somehow win, the land will be too desolated to support us."

"I think still you can spare a few forests," said Van Rijn. "This is not an overpopulated country."

"See here," said Trolwen in a harshening tone, "I've borne with you so far. I admit you're essentially right: that to fare out with all our power, for a decisive battle with the massed enemy, is to risk final destruction. But to sit here, doing nothing but make little guerrilla raids on their outposts, while they grind away our nation—that is to make certain we are doomed."

"We needed time," said Van Rijn. "Time to modify the extra field pieces, making up for what we lost at Mannenach."

"Why? They're not portable, without trains. And to make matters worse that motherless Delp has torn up the rails!"

"Oh, yes, they are portable. My young friend Wace has done a little redesigning. Knocked down, with females and cubs to help, everyone carrying a single small piece or two—we can tote a heavy battery of weapons, by damn!"

"I know. You've explained all this before. And I repeat: what will we use them against? If we set them up at some particular spot, the Lannachska need only avoid that spot. And we can't stay very long in any one place, because our numbers eat it baren." Trolwen drew a breath. "I did not come here to argue, Eart'a. I came from the General Council of Lannach, to tell you that Salmenbrok's food is exhausted—and so is the army's patience. We *must* go out and fight!"

"We shall," said Van Rijn imperturbably. "Come, I will go talk at these puff-head councilors."

He stuck his head in the door: "Wace, boy, best you start to pack what we have. Soon we transport it."

"I heard you," said the younger man.

"Good. You make the work here, I make the politicking, so it goes along fine, *nie?*" Van Rijn rubbed shaggy fists, beamed, and shuffled off with Trolwen and Tolk.

Wace stared after him, into the blind fog-wall. "Yes," he said. "That's how it has been. We work, and he talks. Very equitable!"

"What do you mean?" Sandra raised her head from the table at which she sat marking gun parts with a small paintbrush. A score of females were working beside her.

"What I said. I wonder why I don't say it to his face.

I'm not afraid of that fat parasite, and I don't want his mucking paycheck any more." Wace waved at the mill and its sooty confusion. "Do this, do that, he says, and then strolls off again. When I think how he's eating food which would keep *you* alive—"

"You do not understand?" She stared at him for a moment. "No, I think maybe you have been too busy, all the time here, to stop and think. And before then, you were a small-job man without the art of government, not?"

"What do you mean?" he echoed her. He regarded her with eyes washed-out and bleared by fatigue.

"Maybe later. Now we must hurry. Soon we will leave this town, and everything must be set to go."

This time she had found a place for her hands, in the ten or fifteen Earth-days since Mannenach. Van Rijn had demanded that everything—the excess war materièl, which there had luckily not been room enough to take down to battle—be made portable by air. That involved a certain amount of modification, so that the large wooden members could be cut up into smaller units, for reassembly where needed. Wace had managed that. But it would all be one chaos at journey's end, unless there was a system for identifying each item. Sandra had devised the markings and was painting them on.

Neither she nor Wace had stopped for much sleep. They had not even paused to wonder greatly what use there would be for their labor.

"Old Nick did say something about attacking the Fleet itself," muttered Wace. "Has he gone uncon?

Are we supposed to land on the water and assemble our catapults?''

"Perhaps," said Sandra. Her tone was serene. "I do not worry so much any more. Soon it will be all decided because we have food for just four Earth-weeks or less."

"We can last at least two months without eating at all," he said.

"But we will be weak." She dropped her gaze. "Eric—"

"Yes?" He left his mill-powered obsidian-toothed circular saw, and came over to stand above her. The dull rush light caught drops of fog in her hair, they gleamed like tiny jewels.

"Soon . . . it will make no matter what I do . . . there will be hard work, needing strength and skill I have not . . . maybe fighting, where I am only one more bow, not a very strong bow even." Her finger-nails whitened where she gripped her brush. "So when it comes to that, I will eat no more. You and Nicholas take my share."

"Don't be a fool," he said hoarsely.

She sat up straight, turned around and glared at him. Her pale cheeks reddened. "Do you not be the fool, Eric Wace," she snapped. "If I can give you and him just one extra week where you are strong—where your hunger does not keep you from even thinking clearly— then it will be myself I save too, perhaps. And if not, I have only lost one or two worthless weeks. Now get back to your machine!"

He watched her, for some small while, and his heart

thuttered. Then he nodded and returned to his own work.

And down the trails to an open place of harsh grass, where the Council sat on a cliff's edge, Van Rijn picked his steadily swearing way.

The elders of Lannach lay like sphinxes against a skyline gone formless gray, and waited for him. Trolwen went to the head of the double line, Tolk remained by the human.

"In the name of the All-Wise, we are met," said the commander ritually. "Let sun and moons illumine our minds. Let the ghosts of our grandmothers lend us their guidance. May I not shame those who flew before me, nor those who come after." He relaxed a trifly. "Well, my officers, it's decided we can't stay here. I've brought the Eart'a to advise us. Will you explain the alternatives to him?"

A gaunt, angry-eyed old Lannacha hunched his wings and spat: "First, Flockchief, why is he here at all?"

"By the commander's invitation," said Tolk smoothly.

"I mean . . . Herald, let's not twist words. You know what I mean. The Mannenach expedition was undertaken at his urging. It cost us the worst defeat in our history. Since then, he has insisted our main body stay here, idle, while the enemy ravages an undefended land. I don't see why we should take his advice."

Trolwen's eyes were troubled. "Are there further challenges?" he asked, in a very low voice.

An indignant mumble went down the lines. *"Yes yes . . . yes . . . let him answer, if he can."*

Van Rijn turned turkey red and began to swell like a frog.

"The Eart'a has been challenged in Council," said Trolwen. "Does he wish to reply?"

He sat back then, waiting like the others.

Van Rijn exploded.

"Pest and damnation! Four million worms cocooning in hell! How long am I to be saddled with stupid ungratefuls? How many politicians and brass hats have You Up There plagued this universe with?" He waved his fists in the air and screamed. "Satan and sulfur! It is not to be stood! If you are all so hot to make suicides for yourselves, why does poor old Van Rijn have to hold on to your coat tails all the time? *Perbacco,* you stop insulting me or I stuff you down your own throats!" He advanced like a moving mountain, roaring at them. The nearest councilors flinched away.

"Eart'a . . . sir . . . officer . . . please!" whispered Trolwen.

When he had them sufficiently browbeaten, Van Rijn said coldly: "All rights. I tell you, by damn. I give you good advices and you stupid them up and blame me—but I am a poor patient old man, not like when I was young and strong no, I suffer it with Christian meekness and keep on giving you good advices.

"I warned you and I warned you, do not hit Mannenach first, I warned you. I told you the rafts could come right up to its walls, and the rafts are the strength of the Fleet. I got down on these two poor old knees, begging and pleading with you first to take the key upland towns, but no, you would not listen to me. And still we *had* Mannenach, but the victory was stupided away . . . oh, if I had wings like an angel, so I could have led you in person! I would be cock-a-doodle-dooing on the admiral's masthead this moment, by holy Nicolai miter! That is why you take my advices, by damn—no, you take my orders! No more backward talking from you, or I wash my hands with you and make my own way home. From now on, if you want to keep living, when Van Rijn says frog, you jump. Understanding?''

He paused. He could hear his own asthmatic wheezes . . . and the far unhappy mumble of the camp, and the cold wet clinking of water down alien rocks nothing more in all the world.

Finally Trolwen said in a weak voice: ''If . . . if the challenge is considered answered . . . we shall resume our business.''

No one spoke.

''Will the Eart'a take the word?'' asked Tolk at last. He alone appeared self-possessed, in the critical glow of one who appreciates fine acting.

''*Ja*. I will say, I know we cannot remain here any more. You ask why I kept the army on leash and let Captain Delp have his way.'' Van Rijn ticked it off on his fingers. ''*Imprimis,* to attack him directly is what he wants: he can most likely beat us, since his force is bigger and not so hungry or discouraged. *Secundus,* he will not advance to Salmenbrok while we are all here, since we could bushwhack him; therefore, by staying put the army has gained me a chance to make ready our artillery pieces. *Tertius,* it is my hope that by all this delay while I had the mill going, we have won the means of victory.''

"What?" It barked from the throat of a councilor who forgot formalities.

"Ah." Van Rijn laid a finger to his imposing nose and winked. "We shall see. Maybe now you think even if I am a pitiful old weak tired man who should be in bed with hot toddies and a good cigar, still a Polesotechnic merchant is not just to sneeze at. So? Well, then. I propose we all leave this land and head north."

A hubbub broke loose. He waited patiently for it to subside.

"Order!" shouted Trolwen. "Order!" He slapped the hard earth with his tail. "Quiet, there, officers! Eart'a, there has been some talk of abandoning Lannach altogether—more and more of it, indeed, as our folk lose heart. We could still reach Swampy Kilnu in time to . . . to save most of our females and cubs at Birthtime. But it would be to give up our towns, our fields and forests—everything we have, everything our forebears labored for hundreds of years to create—to sink back into savagery, in a dark fever-haunted jungle, to become nothing—I myself will die in battle before making such a choice."

He drew a breath and hurled out: "But Kilnu is, at least, to the south. North of Achan, there is still ice!"

"Just so," said Van Rijn.

"Would you have us starve and freeze on the Dawrnach glaciers? We can't land any further south than Drawrnach; the Fleet's scouts would be certain to spot us anywhere in Holmenach. Unless you want to fight the last fight in the archipelago—?"

"No," said Van Rijn. "We should sneak up to this Dawrnach place. We can pack a lunch—take maybe a ten-days' worth of food and fuel with us, as well as the armament—*nie?*''

"Well . . . yes . . . but even so—Are you suggesting we should attack the Fleet itself, the rafts, from the north? It would be an unexpected direction. But it would be just as hopeless.''

"Surprise we will need for my plan,'' said Van Rijn. "*Ja.* We cannot tell the army. One of them might be captured in some skirmish and made to tell the Drak'honai. Best maybe I not even tell you.''

"Enough!'' said Trolwen. "Let me hear your scheme.''

Much later: "It won't work. Oh, it might well be technically feasible. But it's a political impossibility.''

"Politics!'' groaned Van Rijn. "What is it this time?.''

"The warriors . . . yes, and the females too, even the cubs, since it would be our whole nation which goes to Dawrnach. They must be told why we do so. Yet the whole scheme, as you admit, will be ruined if one person falls into enemy hands and tells what he knows under torture.''

"But he need not know,'' said Van Rijn. "All he need be told is, we spend a little while gathering food and wood to travel with. Then we are to pack up and go some other place, he has not been told where or why.''

"We are not Drakska,'' said Trolwen angrily. "We are a free folk. I have no right to make so important a decision without submitting it to a vote.''

"Hm-m-m maybe you could talk to them?'' Van Rijn tugged his mustaches. "Orate at them. Persuade them to waive their right to know and help decide. Talk them into following you with no questions.''

"No," said Tolk. "I'm a specialist in the arts of persuasion, Eart'a, and I've measured the limits of those arts. We deal less with a Flock now than a mob—cold, hungry, without hope, without faith in its leaders, ready to give up everything—or rush forth to blind battle—they haven't the morale to follow anyone into an unknown venture.''

"Morale can be pumped in," said Van Rijn. "I will try."

You!''

"I am not so bad at oratings, myself, when there is need. Let me address them.''

"They . . . they—'' Tolk stared at him. Then he laughed, a jarringly sarcastic note. "Let it be done, Flockchief. Let's hear what words this Eart'a can find, so much better than our own.''

And an hour later, he sat on a bluff, with his people a mass of shadow below him, and he heard Van Rijn bass come through the fog like thunder:

''. . . I say only, think what you have here, and what they would take away from you:

*"This royal throne of kings, this
sceptr'd isle,
This earth of majesty, this seat of
Mars,
This other Eden, demi-paradise,
This fortress built by Nature for
herself*

*Against infection and the hand of
war,
This happy breed ..."*

"I don't comprehend all those words," whispered
Tolk.

"Be still!" answered Trolwen. "Let me hear."
There were tears in his eyes; he shivered.

"... *This blessed plot, this earth, this realm, this
Lannach* ..."

The army beat its wings and screamed.

Van Rijn continued through adaptations of Pericles'
funeral speech, "Scots Wha' Hae," and the Gettys-
burg Address. By the time he had finished discussing
St. Crispin's Day, he could have been elected commander if he chose.

XVI

The island called Dawrnach lay well beyond the archipelago's end, several hundred kilometers north of Lannach. However swiftly the Flock flew, with pauses for rest on some bird-shrieking skerry, it was a matter of Earth-days to get there, and a physical nightmare for humans trussed in carrying nets. Afterward Wace's recollections of the trip were dim.

When he stood on the beach at their goal, his legs barely supporting him, it was small comfort.

High Summer had come here also, and this was not too far north; still, the air remained wintry and Tolk said no one had ever tried to live here. The Holmenach islands deflected a cold current out of The Ocean, up into the Iceberg Sea, and those bitter waters flowed around Dawrnach.

Now the Flock, wings and wings and wings dropping down from the sky until they hid its roiling grayness, had reached journey's conclusion: black sands, washed by heavy dark tides and climbing sheer up through permanent glaciers to the inflamed throat of a volcano. Thin straight trees were sprinkled over the lower slopes, between quaking tussocks, there were a few sea birds, to dip above the broken offshore ice-floes; otherwise the hidden sun threw its clotted-blood light on a sterile country.

Sandra shuddered. Wace was shocked to see how thin she had already grown. And now that they were here, in the last phase of their striving—belike of their lives—she intended to eat no more.

She wrapped her stinking coarse jacket more tightly about her. The wind caught snarled pale elflocks of her hair and fluttered them forlorn against black igneous cliffs. Around her crouched, walked, wriggled, and flapped ten thousand angry dragons: whistles and gutturals of unhuman speech, the cannon-crack of leathery wings, overrode the empty wind-whimper. As she rubbed her eyes, pathetically like a child, Wace saw that her once beautiful hands were bleeding where they had clung to the net, and that she shook with weariness.

He felt his heart twisted, and moved toward her. Nicholas van Rijn got there first, fat and greasy, with a roar for comfort: "So, by jolly damn, now we are here and soon I get you home again to a hot bath. Holy St. Dismas, right now I smell you three kilometers up-wind!"

Lady Sandra Tamarin, heiress to the Grand Duchy of

Hermes, gave him a ghostly smile. "If I could rest for a little—" she whispered.

"*Ja, ja,* we see." Van Rijn stuck two fingers in his mouth and let out an eardrum-breaking blast. It caught Trolwen's attention. "You there! Find her here a cave or something and tuck her in."

"I?" Trolwen bridled. "I have the Flock to see to!"

"You heard me, pot head." Van Rijn stumped off and buttonholed Wace. "Now, then. You are ready to begin work? Round up your crew, however many you need to start."

"I—" Wace backed away. "Look here, it's been I don't know how many hours since our last stop, and—"

Van Rijn spat. "And how many weeks makes it since *I* had a smoke or even so much a little glass Genever, ha? You have no considerations for other people." He pointed his beak heavenward and screamed: "Do I have to do everything? Why have You Up There filled up the galaxy with no-good loafers? It is not to be stood!"

"Well ...well—" Wace saw Trolwen leading Sandra off, to find a place where she could sleep, forgetting cold and pain and loneliness for a few niggard hours. He struck a fist into his palm and said: "All right! But what will you be doing?"

"I must organize things, by damn. First I see Trolwen about a gang to cut trees and make masts and yards and oars. Meanwhiles all this canvas we have brought along has got to somehow be made in sails; and there are the riggings; and also we must fix up for eating and shelter— Bah! These is all details. It is not right I should be bothered. Details, I hire ones like you for."

"Is life anything but details?" snapped Wace.

Van Rijn's small gray eyes studied him for a moment. "So," rumbled the merchant, "it gives back talks from you too, ha? You think maybe just because I am old and weak, and do not stand so much the hardships like when I was young . . . maybe I only leech off your work, *nie?* Now is too small time for beating sense into your head. Maybe you learn for yourself." He snapped his fingers. "Jump!"

Wace went off, damning himself for not giving the old pig a fist in the stomach. He would, too, come the day! Not now . . . unfortunately, Van Rijn had somehow oozed into a position where it was him the Lannachska looked up to . . . instead of Wace, who did the actual work—Was that a paranoid thought? No.

Take this matter of the ships, for instance. Van Rijn had pointed out that an island like Dawrnach, loaded with pack ice and calving glaciers, afforded plenty of building material. Stone chisels would shape a vessel as big as any raft in the Fleet, in a few hours' work. The most primitive kind of blowtorch, an oil lamp with a bellows, would smooth it off. A crude mast and rudder could be planted in holes cut for the purpose: water, refreezing, would be a strong cement. With most of the Flock, males, females, old, young, made one enormous labor force for the project, a flotilla comparable in numbers to the whole Fleet could be made in a week.

If an engineer figured out all the practical procedure. How deep a hole to step your mast in? Is ballast needed?

Just how do you make a nice clean cut in an irregular ice block hundreds of meters long? How about smoothing the bottom to reduce drag? The material was rather friable; it could be strengthened considerably by dashing bucketsful of mixed sawdust and sea water over the finished hull, letting this freeze as a kind of armor—but what proportions?

There was no time to really test these things. Somehow, by God and by guess, with every element against him, Eric Wace was expected to produce.

And Van Rijn? What did Van Rijn contribute? The basic idea, airily tossed off, apparently on the assumption that Wace was Aladdin's jinni. Oh, it was quite a flash of imaginative insight, no one could deny that. But imagination is cheap.

Anyone can say: "What we need is a new weapon, and we can make it from such-and-such unprecedented materials." But it will remain an idle fantasy until somebody shows up who can figure out *how* to make the needed weapon.

So, having enslaved his engineer, Van Rijn strolled around, jollying some of the Flock and bullying some of the others—and when he had them all working their idiotic heads off, he rolled up in a blanket and went to sleep!

XVII

Wace stood on the deck of the *Rijstaffel* and watched his enemy come over the world's rim.

Slowly, he reached into the pouch at his side. His hand closed on a chunk of stale bread and a slab of sausage. It was the last Terrestrial food remaining: for Earth-days, now, he had gone on a still thinner ration than before, so that he could enter this battle with something in his stomach.

He found that he didn't want it after all.

Surprisingly little cold breathed up from underfoot. The warm air over the Sea of Achan wafted the ice-chill away. He was less astonished that there had been no appreciable melting in the week he estimated they had been creeping southward; he knew the thermal properties of water.

Behind him, primitive square sails, lashed to yard-arms of green wood on overstrained one-piece masts, bellied in the north wind. These ice ships were tubby, but considerably less so than a Drak'ho raft; and with some unbelievable talent for tyranny, Van Rijn had gotten reluctant Lannachska to work under frigid sea water, cutting the bottoms into a vaguely streamlined shape. Now, given the power of a Diomedean breeze, Lannach's war fleet waddled through Achan waves at a good five knots.

Though the hardest moment, Wace reflected, had not been while they worked their hearts out to finish the craft. It had come afterward, when they were almost ready to leave and the winds turned contrary. For a period measured in Earth-days, thousands of Lannachska huddled soul-sick under freezing rains, ranging after fish and bird rookeries to feed cubs that cried with hunger. Councilors and clan leaders had argued that this was a war on the Fates: there could be no choice but to give up and seek out Swampy Kilnu. Somehow, blustering, shining, pleading, promising—in a few cases, bribing, with what he had won at dice—Van Rijn had held them on Dawrnach.

Well—it was over with.

The merchant came out of the little stone cabin, walked over the gravelstrewn deck past crouching war-engines and heaped missiles, till he reached the bows where Wace stood.

"Best you eat," he said. "Soon gives no chance."

"I'm not hungry," said Wace.

"So, no?" Van Rijn grabbed the sandwich out of his

fingers. "Then, by damn, I am!" He began cramming it between his teeth.

Once again he wore a double set of armor, but he had chosen one weapon only for this occasion, an outsize stone ax with a meter-long handle. Wace carried a smaller tomahawk and a shield. Around the humans, it bristled with armed Lannacska.

"They're making ready to receive us, all right," said Wace. His eyes sought out the gaunt enemy war-canoes, beating upwind.

"You expected a carpet with acres and acres, like they say in America? I bet you they spotted us from the air hours ago. Now they send messengers hurry-like back to their army in Lannach." Van Rijn held up the last fragment of meat, kissed it reverently, and ate it.

Wace's eyes traveled backward. This was the flagship—chosen as such when it turned out to be the fastest—and had the forward position in a long wedge. Several score grayish-white, ragged-sailed, helter-skelter little vessels wallowed after. They were out-numbered and outgunned by the Drak'ho rafts, of course; they just had to hope the odds weren't too great. The much lower freeboard did not matter to a winged race, but it would be important that their crews were not very skilled sailors—

But at least the Lannachska were fighters. Winged tigers by now, thought Wace. The southward voyage had rested them, and trawling had provided the means to feed them, and the will to battle had kindled again. Also, though they had a smaller navy, they probably had more warriors, even counting Delp's absent army.

And they could afford to be reckless. Their females and young were still on Dawrnach—with Sandra, grown so white and quiet—and they had no treasures along to worry about. For cargo they bore just their weapons and their hate.

From the clouds of air-borne, Tolk the Herald came down. He braked on extended wings, slithered to a landing, and curved back his neck swan-fashion to regard the humans.

"Does it all go well down here?" he asked.

"As well as may be," said Van Rijn. "Are we still bearing on the pest-rotten Fleet?"

"Yes. It's not many buaska away now. Barely over your sea-level horizon, in fact; you'll raise it soon. They're using sail and oars alike, trying to get out of our path, but they'll not achieve it if we keep this wind and those canoes don't delay us."

"No sign of the army in Lannach?"

"None yet. I daresay what's-his-name . . . the new admiral that we heard about from those prisoners . . . has messengers scouring the mountains. But that's a big land up there. It will take time to locate him." Tolk snorted professional scorn. "Now *I* would have had constant liaison, a steady two-way flow of Whistlers."

"Still," said Van Rijn, "we must expect them soon, and then gives hell's safety valve popping off."

"Are you certain we can—"

"I am certain of nothings. Now get back to Trolwen and oversee."

Tolk nodded and hit the air again.

Dark purplish water curled in white feathers, beneath

a high heaven where clouds ran like playful mountains, tinted rosy by the sun. Not many kilometers off, a small island rose sheer; through a telescope, Wace could count the patches of yellow blossom nodding under tall bluish conifers. A pair of young Whistlers dipped and soared over his head, dancing like the gay clan banners being unfurled in the sky. It was hard to understand that the slim carved boats racing so near bore fire and sharpened stones.

"Well," said Van Rijn, "here begins our fun. Good St. Dismas, stand by me now."

"St. George would be a little more appropriate, wouldn't he?" asked Wace.

"You may think so. Me, I am too old and fat and cowardly to call on Michael or George or Olaf or any like those soldierly fellows. I feel more at home, me, with saints not so bloody energetic, Dismas or my own good namesake who is so kind to travelers."

"And is also the patron of highway men," remarked Wace. He wished his tongue wouldn't get so thick and dry on him. He felt remote, somehow . . . not really afraid . . . but his knees were rubbery.

"Ha!" boomed Van Rijn. "Good shootings, boy!"

The forward ballista on the *Rijstaffel*, with a whine and a thump, had smacked a half-ton stone into the nearest canoe. The boat cracked like a twig; its crew whirled up, a squad from Trolwen's aerial command pounced, there was a moment's murderous confusion and then the Drak'honai had stopped existing.

Van Rijn grabbed the astonished ballista captain by the hands and danced him over the deck, bawling out,

"Du bist mein Sonnenschein, mein einzig Sonnenschein, du machst mir freulich—"

Another canoe swung about, close-hauled. Wace saw its flamethrower crew bent over their engine and hurled himself flat under the low wall surrounding the ice deck.

The burning stream hit that wall, splashed back, and spread itself on the sea. It could not kindle frozen water, nor melt enough of it to notice. Sheltered amidships, a hundred Lannacha archers sent an arrow-sleet up, to arc under heaven and come down on the canoe.

Wace peered over the wall. The flamethrower pumpman seemed dead, the hoseman was preoccupied with a transfixed wing . . . no steersman either, the canoe's boom slatted about in a meaningless arc while its crew huddled— "Dead ahead!" he roared. "Ram them!"

The Lannacha ship trampled the dugout underfoot.

Drak'ho canoes circled like wolves around a buffalo herd, using their speed and maneuverability. Several darted between ice vessels, to assail from the rear; others went past the ends of the wedge formation. It was not quite a one-sided battle—arrows, catapult bolts, flung stones, all hurt Lannachska; oil jugs arced across the water, exploding on ice decks; now and then a fire stream ignited a sail.

But winged creatures with a few buckets could douse burning canvas. During all that phase of the engagement, only one Lannacha craft was wholly dismasted, and its crew simply abandoned it, parceling themselves out among other vessels. Nothing else could catch fire, except live flesh, which has always been the cheapest article in war.

Several canoes, converging on a single ship, tried to board. They were nonetheless outnumbered, and paid heavily for the attempt. Meanwhile Trolwen, with absolute air mastery, swooped and shot and hammered.

Drak'ho canoes scarcely hindered the attack. The dugouts were rammed, broken, set afire, brushed aside by their unsinkable enemy.

By virtue of being first, of having more or less punched through the line, the *Rijstaffel* met little opposition. What there was, was beaten off by catapult, ballista, fire pot, and arrows: long-range gunnery. The sea itself burned and smoked behind; ahead lay the great rafts.

When those sails and banners came into view, Wace's dragon crewmen began to sing the victory song of the Flock.

"A little premature, aren't they?" he cried above the racket.

"Ah," said Van Rijn quietly, "let them make fun now. So many will soon be down, blind among the fishes, *nie?*"

"I suppose—" Hastily, as if afraid of what he had done merely to save his own life, Wace said; "I like that melody, don't you? It's rather like some old American folk songs. *John Harty,* say."

"Folk songs is all right if you should want to play you are Folk in great big capitals," snorted Van Rijn. "I stick with Mozart, by damn."

He stared down into the water, and a curious wistfulness tinged his voice. "I always hoped maybe I would understand Bach some day, before I die, old Johann Sebastian who talked with God in mathematics. I have not the brains, though, in this dumb old head. So maybe I ask only one more chance to listen at *Eine Kleine Nacht-musik*."

There was an uproar in the Fleet. Slowly and ponderously, churning the sea with spider-leg oars, the rafts were giving up their attempt at evasion. They were pulling into war formation.

Van Rijn waved angrily at a Whistler. "Quick! You get upstairs fast, and tell that crockhead Trolwen not to bother air-covering us against the canoes. Have him attack the rafts. Keep them busy, by hell! Don't let messengers flappity-flip between enemy captains so they can organize!"

As the young Lannacha streaked away, the merchant tugged his goatee—almost lost by now in a dirt-stiffened beard—and snarled: "Great hairy honeypots! How long do I have to do all the thinkings? Good St. Nicholas, you bring me an officer staff with brains between the ears, instead of clabbered oatmeal, and I build you a cathedral on Mars! You hear me?"

"Trolwen is in the midst of a fight up there," protested Wace. "You can't expect him to think of everything."

"Maybe not," conceded Van Rijn grudgingly. "Maybe I am the only one in all the galaxy who makes no mistakes."

Horribly near, the massed rafts became a storm when Trolwen took his advice. Bat-winged devils sought each other's lives through one red chaos. Wace thought his own ships' advance must be nearly unnoticed in that whirling, shrieking destruction.

"They're *not* getting integrated!" he said, beating his fist on the wall. "Before God, they're not!"

A Whistler landed, coughing blood; there was a monstrous bruise on his side. "Over there . . . Tolk the Herald says . . . empty spot . . . drive wedge in Fleet—" The thin body arced and then slid inertly to the deck. Wace stooped, taking the unhuman youth in his arms. He heard blood gurgle in lungs pierced by the broken ends of ribs.

"Mother, mother," gasped the Whistler. "He hit me with an ax. Make it stop hurting, mother."

Presently he died.

Van Rijn cursed his awkward vessel into a course change—not more than a few degrees, it wasn't capable of more, but as the nearer rafts began to loom above the ice deck, it could be seen that there was a wide gap in their line. Trolwen's assault had so far prevented its being closed. Redstained water, littered with dropped spears and bows, pointed like a hand toward the admiral's floating castle.

"In there!" bawled Van Rijn. "Clobber them! Eat them for breakfast!"

A catapult bolt came whirring over the wall, ripped through his sleeve and showered ice chips where it struck. Then three streams of liquid fire converged on the *Rijstaffel*.

Flame fingers groped their way across the deck, one Lannacha lay screaming and charring where they had touched him, and found the sails. It was no use to pour water this time: oil-drenched, mast and rigging and canvas became one great torch.

Van Rijn left the helmsman he had been swearing at and bounded across the deck, slipped where some of it had melted, skated on his broad bottom till he fetched up against a wall, and crawled back to his feet calling down damnation on the cosmos. Up to the starboard shrouds he limped, and his stone ax began gnawing the cordage. "Here!" he yelled. "Fast! Help me, you jelly-bones! Quick, have you got fur on the brain, quick before we drift past!"

Wace, directing the ballista crew, which was stoning a nearby raft, understood only vaguely. Others were more ready than he. They swarmed to Van Rijn and hewed. He himself sought the racked oil bombs and broke one at the foot of the burning mast.

Its socket melted, held up only by the shrouds, the enormous torch fell to port when the starboard lines were slashed. It struck the raft there; flames ran from it, beating back frantic Drak'ho crewmen who would push it loose; rigging caught; timbers began to char. As the *Rijstaffel* drifted away, that enemy vessel turned into a single bellowing pyre.

Now the ice ship was nearly uncontrollable, driven by momentum and chance currents deeper into the confused Fleet. But through the gap which Van Rijn had so ardently widened, the rest of the Lannacha craft pushed. War-flames raged between floating monsters —but wood will burn and ice will not.

Through a growing smoke-haze, among darts and

arrows that rattled down from above, on a deck strewn with dead and hurt but still filled by the revengeful hale, Wace trod to the nearest bomb crew. They were preparing to ignite another raft as soon as the ship's drift brought them into range.

"No," he said.

"What?" The captain turned a sooty face to him, crest adroop with weariness. "But sir, they'll be pumping fire at us!"

"We can stand that," said Wace. "We're pretty well sheltered by our walls. I don't want to burn that raft. I want to capture it!"

The Diomedean whistled. Then his wings spread and his eyes flared and he asked: "May I be the first on board it?"

Van Rijn passed by, hefting his ax. He could not have heard what was said, but he rumbled: "*Ja*. I was just about to order this. We can use us a transportation that maneuvers."

The word went over the ship. Its slippery deck darkened with armed shapes that waited. Closer and closer, the wrought ice-floe bore down on the higher and more massive raft. Fire, stones, and quarrels reached out for the Lannachska. They endured it, grimly. Wace sent a Whistler up to Trolwen to ask for help; a flying detachment silenced the Drak'ho artillery with arrows.

Trolwen still had overwhelming numerical superiority. He could choke the sky with his warriors, pinning the Drak'honai to their decks to await sea-borne assault. So far, thought Wace, Diomedes' miserly gods had been smiling on him. It couldn't last much longer.

He followed the first Lannacha wave, which had flown to clear a bridgehead on the raft. He sprang from the ice-floe when it bumped to a halt, grasped a massive timber, and scrambled up the side. When he reached the top and unlimbered his tomahawk and shield, he found himself in a line of warriors. Smoke from the burnings elsewhere stung his eyes; only indistinctly did he see the defending Drak'honai, pulled into ranks ahead of him and up on the higher decks.

Had the yelling and tumbling about overhead suddenly redoubled?

A stumpy finger tapped him. He turned around to meet Van Rijn's porcine gaze.

"Whoof and whoo! What for a climb that was! Better I should have stayed, *nie?* Well, boy, we are on our own now. Tolk just sent me word, the whole Drak'ho Expeditionary Force is in sight and lolloping hereward fast."

XVIII

Briefly, Wace felt sick. Had it all come to this, a chipped flint in his skull after Delp's army had beaten off the Lannachska?

Then he remembered standing on the cold black beach of Dawrnach, shortly before they sailed, and wondering aloud if he would ever again speak with Sandra. "I'll have the easy part if we lose," he had said. "It'll be over quickly enough for me. But you—"

She gave him a look that brimmed with pride, and answered: "What makes you think you can lose?"

He hefted his weapon. The lean winged bodies about him hissed, bristled, and glided ahead.

These were mostly troopers from the Mannenach attempt; every ice ship bore a fair number who had been taught the elements of ground fighting. And on the whole trip south to find the Fleet, Van Rijn and the Lannacha captains had exhorted them: "Do not join our aerial forces. Stay on the decks when we board a raft. This whole plan hinges on how many rafts we can seize or destroy. Trolwen and his air squadrons will merely be up there to support *you*."

The idea took root reluctantly in any Diomedean brain. Wace was not at all certain it wouldn't die within the next hour, leaving him and Van Rijn marooned on hostile timbers while their comrades soared up to a pointless sky battle. But he had no choice, save to trust them now.

He broke into a run. The screech that his followers let out tore at his eardrums.

Wings threshed before him. Instinctively, the untrained Drak'ho lines were breaking up. Through geological eras, the only sane thing for a Diomedean to do had been to get above an attacker. Wace stormed on where they had stood.

Lifting from all the raft, enemy sailors stooped on these curious unflying adversaries. A Lannacha forgot himself, flapped up, and was struck by three meteor bodies. He was hurled like a broken puppet into the sea. The Drak'honai rushed downward.

And they met spears which snapped up like a picket fence. No few of Lannach's one-time ground troopers had rescued their basketwork shields from the last retreat and were now again transformed into artificial turtles. The rest fended off the aerial assault—and the archers made ready.

Wace heard the sinister whistle rise behind him, and saw fifty Drak'honai fall.

Then a dragon roared in his face, striking with a knife-toothed rake. Wace caught the blow on his shield. It shuddered in his left arm, numbing the muscles. He lashed out a heavy-shod foot, caught the hard belly and heard the wind leave the Drak'ho. His tomahawk rose and fell with a dull chopping sound. The Diomedean fluttered away, pawing at a broken wing.

Wace hurried on. The Drak'honai, stunned by the boarding party's tactics, were now milling around overhead out of bowshot. Females snarled in the forecastle doors, spreading wings to defend their screaming cubs. They were ignored: the object was to capture the raft's artillery.

Someone up there must have seen what was intended. His hawk-shriek and hawk-stoop were ended by a Lannacha arrow; but then an organized line peeled off the Drak'honai mass, plummeted to the forecastle deck, and took stance before the main battery of flamethrowers and ballistae.

"So!" rumbled Van Rijn. "They make happy fun games after all. We see about this!"

He broke into an elephantine trot, whirling the great mallet over his head. A slingstone bounced off his leather-decked abdomen, an arrow ripped along one cheek, blowgun darts pincushioned his double cuirass. He got a boost from two winged guards, up the sheer ladderless bulkhead of the forecastle. Then he was in among the defenders.

"*Je maintiendrai!*" he bawled, and stove in the head of the nearest Drak'ho. "*God sent the right!*" he shouted, stamping on the shaft of a rake that clawed after him. *"Fram, fram, Kristmenn, Krossmenn, Kongsmenn!"* he bellowed, drumming on the ribs of three warriors who ramped close. *"Heineken's Bier!"* he trumpeted, turning to wrestle with a winged shape that fastened onto his back, and wringing its neck.

Wace and the Lannachska joined him. There was an interval with hammer and thrust and the huge bone-breaking buffets of wing and tail. The Drak'honai broke. Van Rijn sprang to the flamethrower and pumped. "Aim the hose!" he panted. "Flush them out, you bat-infested heads!" A gleeful Lannacha seized the ceramic nozzle, pressed the hardwood ignition piston, and squirted burning oil upward.

Down on the lower decks, ballistae began to thump, catapults sang and other flamethrowers licked. A party from the ice ship reassembled one of their wooden machine guns and poured darts at the last Drak'ho counterassault.

A female shape ran from the forecastle. "It's our husbands they kill!" she shrieked. "Destroy them!"

Van Rijn leaped off the upper deck, a three-meter fall. Planks thundered and groaned when he hit them. Puffing, waving his arms, he got ahead of the frantic creature. "Get back!" he yelled in her own language. "Back inside! Shoo! Scat! Want to leave your cubs unprotected? I eat young Drak'honai! With horse-radish!"

She wailed and scuttled back to shelter. Wace let out a gasp. His skin was sodden with sweat. It had not been too serious a danger, perhaps . . . in theory, a female mob could have been massacred under the eyes of its young . . . but who could bring himself to that? Not Eric Wace, certainly. Better give up and take one's spear thrust like a gentleman.

He realized, then, that the raft was his.

Smoke still thickened the air too much for him to see very well what was going on elsewhere. Now and then, through a breach in it, appeared some vision: a raft set unquenchably afire, abandoned; an ice vessel, cracked, dismasted, arrow-swept, still bleakly slugging it out; another Lannacha ship laying to against a raft, another boarding party; the banner of a Lannacha clan blowing in sudden triumph on a foreign masthead. Wace had no idea how the sea fight as a whole was going—how many ice craft had been raked clean, deserted by discouraged crews, seized by Drak'ho counterattack, left drifting uselessly remote from the enemy.

It had been perfectly clear, he thought—Van Rijn had said it bluntly enough to Trolwen and the Council—that the smaller, less well equipped, virtually untrained Lannacha navy would have no chance whatsoever of decisively whipping the Fleet. The crucial phase of this battle was not going to involve stones or flames.

He looked up. Beyond the spars and lines, where the haze did not reach, heaven lay unbelievably cool. The formations of war, weaving in and about, were so far above him that they looked like darting swallows.

Only after minutes did his inexpert eye grasp the picture.

With most of his force down among the rafts, Trolwen was ridiculously outnumbered in the air as soon as Delp arrived. On the other hand, Delp's folk had been flying for hours to get here; they were no match individually for well-rested Lannachska. Realizing this, each commander used his peculiar advantage: Delp ordered unbreakable mass charges, Trolwen used small squadrons which swooped in, snapped wolfishly, and darted back again. The Lannachska retreated all the time, except when Delp tried to send a large body of warriors down to relieve the rafts. Then the entire, superbly integrated air force at Trolwen's disposal would smash into that body. It would disperse when Delp brought in reinforcements, but it had accomplished its purpose—to break up the formation and checkrein the seaward movement.

So it went, for some timeless time in the wind under the High Summer sun. Wace lost himself, contemplating the terrible beauty of death winged and disciplined. Van Rijn's voice pulled him grudgingly back to luckless unflying humanness.

"Wake up! Are you making dreams, maybe, like you stand there with your teeth hanging out and flapping in the breeze? Lightnings and Lucifer! If we want to keep this raft, we have to make some use with it, by damn. You boss the battery here and I go tell the helmsman what to do. So!" He huffed off, like an ancient steam locomotive in weight and noise and sootiness.

They had beaten off every attempt at recapture, until the expelled crew went wrathfully up to join Delp's legions. Now, awkwardly handling the big sails, or ordered protestingly below to the sweeps, Van Rijn's gang got their new vessel into motion. It grunted its way across a roiled, smoky waste of water, until a Drak'ho craft loomed before it. Then the broadsides cut loose, the arrows went like sleet, and crew locked with crew in troubled air midway between the thuttering rafts.

Wace stood his ground on the foredeck, directing the fire of its banked engines: stones, quarrels, bombs, oil-streams, hurled across a few meters to shower splinters and char wood as they struck. Once he organized a bucket brigade, to put out the fire set by an enemy hit. Once he saw one of his new catapults, and its crew, smashed by a two-ton rock, and forced the survivors to lever that stone into the sea and rejoin the fight. He saw how sails grew tattered, yards sagged drunkenly, bodies heaped themselves on both vessels after each clumsy round. And he wondered, in a dim part of his brain, why life had no more sense, anywhere in the known universe, than to be forever tearing itself.

Van Rijn did not have the quality of crew to win by sheer bombardment, like a neolithic Nelson. Nor did he especially want to try boarding still another craft; it was all his little tyro force could do to man and fight this one. But he pressed stubbornly in, holding the helmsmen to their collision course, going belowdecks himself to keep exhausted Lannachska at their heavy oars. And his raft wallowed its way through a firestorm, a stonestorm, a storm of living bodies, until it was almost on the enemy vessel.

Then horns hooted among the Drak'honai, their

sweeps churned water and they broke from their place in the Fleet's formation to disengage.

Van Rijn let them go, vanishing into the hazed masts and cordage that reached for kilometers around him. He stumped to the nearest hatch, went down through the poopdeck cabins and so out on the main deck. He rubbed his hands and chortled. "Aha! We gave him a little scare, eh, what say? He'll not come near any of our boats soon again, him!"

"I don't understand, councilor," said Angrek, with immense respect. "We had a smaller crew, with far less skill. He ought to have stayed put, or even moved in on us. He could have wiped us out, if we didn't abandon ship altogether."

"Ah!" said Van Rijn. He wagged a sausagelike finger. "But you see, my young and innocent one, he is carrying females and cubs, as well as many valuable tools and other goods. His whole life is on his raft. He dare not risk its destruction; we could so easy set it hopeless afire, even if we can't make capture. Ha! It will be a frosty morning in hell when they outthink Nicholas van Rijn, by damn!"

"Females——" Angrek's eyes shifted to the forecastle. A lickerish light rose in them.

"After all," he murmured, "it's not as if they were *our* females——"

A score or more Lannachska were already drifting in that same direction, elaborately casual—but their wings were held stiff and their tails twitched. It was noteworthy that more of the recent oarsmen were in that group than any other class.

Wace came running to the forecastle's edge. He leaned over it, cupped his hands and shouted: "Freeman van Rijn! Look upstairs!"

"So." The merchant raised pouched little eyes, blinked, sneezed, and blew his craggy nose. One by one, the Lannachska resting on scarred bloody decks lifted their own gaze skyward. And a stillness fell on them.

Up there, the struggle was ending.

Delp had finally assembled his forces into a single irresistible mass and taken them down as a unit to sea level. There they joined the embattled raft crews—one raft at a time. A Lannachska boarding party, so suddenly and grossly outnumbered, had no choice but to flee, abandon even its own ice ship, and go up to Trolwen.

The Drak'honai made only one attempt to recapture a raft which was fully in Lannacha possession. It cost them gruesomely. The classic dictum still held, that purely air-borne forces were relatively impotent against a well-defended unit of the Fleet.

Having settled in this decisive manner exactly who held every single raft, Delp reorganized and led a sizable portion of his troops aloft again to engage Trolwen's augmented air squadrons. If he could clear them away, then, given the craft remaining to Drak'ho plus total sky domination, Delp could regain the lost vessels.

But Trolwen did not clear away so easily. And, while naval fights such as Van Rijn had been waging went on below, a vicious combat traveled through the clouds. Both were indecisive.

Such was the overall view of events, as Tolk related it to the humans an hour or so later. All that could be seen from the water was that the sky armies were separating. They hovered and wheeled, dizzyingly high overhead, two tangled masses of black dots against ruddy-tinged cloud banks. Doubtless threats, curses, and boasts were tossed across the wind between them, but there were no more arrows.

"What is it?" gasped Angrek. "What's happening up there?"

"A truce, of course," said Van Rijn. He picked his teeth with a fingernail, hawked, and patted his abdomen complacently. "They was making nowheres, so finally Tolk got someone through to Delp and said let's talk this over, and Delp agreed."

"But—we can't—you can't bargain with a Draka! He's not . . . he's *alien!*"

A growl of goose-pimpled loathing assent went along the weary groups of Lannachska.

"You can't reason with a filthy wild animal like that," said Angrek. "All you can do is kill it. Or it will kill you!"

Van Rijn cocked a brow at Wace, who stood on the deck above him, and said in Anglic: "I thought maybe we could tell them now that this truce is the only objective of all our fighting so far—but maybe not just yet, *nie?*"

"I wonder if we'll ever dare admit it," said the younger man.

"We will have to admit it, this very day, and hope we do not get stuffed alive with red peppers for what we say. After alls, we did make Trolwen and the Council agree. But then, they are very hard-boiled-egg heads, them.'' Van Rijn shrugged. ''Comes now the talking. So far we have had it soft. This is the times that fry men's souls. Ha! Have you got the nerve to see it through?''

XIX

Approximately one tenth of the rafts lumbered out of the general confusion and assembled a few kilometers away. They were joined by such ice ships as were still in service. The decks of all were jammed with tensely waiting warriors. These were the vessels held by Lannach.

Another tenth or so still burned, or had been torn and beaten by stonefire until they were breaking up under Achan's mild waves. These were the derelicts, abandoned by both nations. Among them were many dugouts, splintered, broken, kindled, or crewed only by dead Drak'honai.

The remainder drew into a mass around the admiral's castle. This was no group of fully manned, fully equipped rafts and canoes; no crew had escaped losses, and a good many vessels were battered nearly into uselessness. If the Fleet could get half their normal fighting strength back into action, they would be very, very lucky.

Nevertheless, this would be almost three times as many units as the Lannachska now held *in toto*. The numbers of males on either side were roughly equal; but, with more cargo space, the Drak'honai had more ammunition. Each of their vessels was also individually superior: better constructed than an ice ship, better crewed than a captured raft.

In short, Drak'ho still held the balance of power.

As he helped Van Rijn down into a seized canoe, Tolk said wryly: "I'd have kept my armor on if I were you, Eart'a. You'll only have to be laced back into it, when the truce ends."

"Ah." The merchant stretched monstrously, puffed out his stomach, and plumped himself down on a seat. "Let us suppose, though, the armistice does not break. Then I will have been wearing that bloody-be-smeared corset all for nothings."

"I notice," added Wace, "neither you nor Trolwen are cuirassed."

The commander smoothed his mahogany fur with a nervous hand. "That's for the dignity of the Flock," he muttered. "Those muck-walkers aren't going to think I'm afraid of them."

The canoe shoved off, its crew bent to the oars, it skipped swiftly over wrinkled dark waters. Above it dipped and soared the rest of the agreed-on Lannacha guard, putting on their best demonstration of parade flying for the edification of the enemy. There were about a hundred all told. It was comfortlessly little to take into the angered Fleet.

"I don't expect to reach any agreement," said Trolwen. "No one can—with a mind as foreign as theirs."

"The Fleet peoples are just like you," said Van Rijn. "What you need is more brotherhood, by damn. You should bash in their heads without this race prejudice."

"Just like *us?*" Trolwen bristled. His eyes grew flat glass-yellow. "See here, Eart'a—"

"Never mind," said Van Rijn. "So they do not have a rutting season. So you think this is a big thing. All right. I got some thinkings to make of my own. Shut up."

The wind ruffled waves and strummed idly on rigging. The sun struck long copper-tinged rays through scudding cloudbanks, to walk on the sea with fiery footprints. The air was cool, damp, smelling a little of salty life. It would not be an easy time to die, thought Wace. Hardest of all, though, to forsake Sandra, where she lay dwindling under the ice cliffs of Dawrnach. *Pray for my soul, beloved, while you wait to follow me. Pray for my soul.*

"Leaving personal feelings aside," said Tolk, "there's much in the commander's remarks. That is, a folk with lives as alien to ours as the Drakska will have minds equally alien. I don't pretend to follow the thoughts of you Eart'ska: I consider you my friends, but let's admit it, we have very little in common. I only trust you because your immediate motive—survival—has been made so clear to me. When I don't quite follow your reasoning, I can safely assume that it is at least well-intentioned.

"But the Drakska, now—how can they be trusted? Let's say that a peace agreement is made. How can we know they'll keep it? They may have no concept of honor at all, just as they lack all concept of sexual decency. Or, even if they do intend to abide by their oaths, are we sure the words of the treaty will mean the same thing to them as to us? In my capacity of Herald, I've seen many semantic misunderstandings between tribes with different languages. So what of tribes with different instincts?

"Or I wonder . . . can we even trust ourselves to keep such a pledge? We do not hate anyone merely for having fought us. But we hate dishonor, perversion, uncleanliness. How can we live with ourselves, if we make peace with creatures whom the gods must loathe?"

He sighed and looked moodily ahead to the nearing rafts.

Wace shrugged. "Has it occurred to you, they are thinking very much the same things about you?" he retorted.

"Of course they are," said Tolk. "That's yet another hailstorm in the path of negotiations."

Personally, thought Wace, *I'll be satisfied with a temporary settlement. Just let them patch up their differences long enough for a message to reach Thursday Landing. (How?) Then they can rip each other's throats out for all I care.*

He glanced around him, at the slim winged forms, and thought of work and war, torment and triumph— yes, and now and then some laughter or a fragment of song—shared. He thought of high-hearted Trolwen, philosophic Tolk, earnest young Angrek, he thought of brave kindly Delp and his wife Rondonis, who was so much more a lady than many a human female he had known. And the small furry cubs which tumbled in the dust or climbed into his lap . . . No, he told himself, *I'm wrong. It means a great deal to me, after all, that this war should be permanently ended*.

The canoe slipped in between towering raft walls. Drak'ho faces looked stonily down on it. Now and then someone spat into its wake. They were all very quiet.

The unwieldy pile of the flagship loomed ahead. There were banners strung from the mastheads, and a guard in bright regalia formed a ring enclosing the main deck. Just before the wooden castle, sprawled on furs and cushions, Admiral T'heonax and his advisory council waited. To one side stood Captain Delp with a few personal guards, in war-harness still sweaty and unkempt.

Total silence lay over them as the canoe came to a halt and made fast to a bollard. Trolwen, Tolk, and most of the Lannacha troopers flew straight up to the deck. It was minutes later, after much pushing, panting, and swearing, that the humans topped that mountainous hull.

Van Rijn glowered about him. "What for hospitality!" he snorted in the Drak'ho language. "Not so much as one little rope let down to me, who is pushing my poor old tired bones to an early grave all for your sakes. Before Heaven, it is hard! It is hard! Sometimes I think I give up, me, and retire. Then where will the galaxy be? Then you will all be sorry, when it is too late."

T'heonax gave him a sardonic stare. "You were not the best-behaved guest the Fleet has had, Eart'ho," he answered. "I've a great deal to repay you. Yes. I have not forgotten."

Van Rijn wheezed across the planks to Delp, extending his hand. "So our intelligences was right, and it was you doing all the works," he blared. "I might have been sure. Nobody else in this Fleet has so much near a gram of brains. I, Nicholas van Rijn, compliment you with regards."

T'heonax stiffened and his councilors, rigid in braid and sash, looked duly shocked at this ignoring of the admiral. Delp hung back for an instant. Then he took Van Rijn's hand and squeezed it, quite in the Terrestrial manner.

"Lodestar help me, it is good to see your villanous fat face again," he said. "Do you know how nearly you cost me my . . . everything? Were it not for my lady—"

"Business and friendship we do not mix," said Van Rijn airily. "Ah, yes, good Vrouw Rodonis. How is she and all the little ones? Do they still remember old Uncle Nicholas and the bedtime stories he was telling them, like about the—"

"If you please," said T'heonax in an elaborate voice, "we will, with your permission, carry on. Who

shall interpret? Yes, I remember you now, Herald."
An ugly look. "Your attention, then. Tell your leader
that this parley was arranged by my field commander,
Delp hyr Orikan, without even sending a messenger
down here to consult me. I would have opposed it had I
known. It was neither prudent nor necessary. I shall
have to have these decks scrubbed where barbarians
have trod. However, since the Fleet is bound by its
honor—you do have a word for honor in your language,
don't you?—I will hear what your leader has to say."

Tolk nodded curtly and put it into Lannachamael.
Trolwen sat up, eyes kindling. His guards growled,
their hands tightened on their weapons. Delp shuffled
his feet unhappily, and some of T'heonax's captains
looked away in an embarrassed fashion.

"Tell him," said Trolwen after a moment, with
bitter precision, "that we will let the Fleet depart from
Achan at once. Of course, we shall want hostages."

Tolk translated. T'heonax peeled lips back from
teeth and laughed. "They sit here with their wretched
handful of rafts and say this to us?" His courtiers
tittered an echo.

But his councilors, who captained his flotillas, remained grave. It was Delp who stepped forward and
said: "The admiral knows I have taken my share in this
war. With these hands, wings, this tail, I have killed
enemy males; with these teeth, I have drawn enemy
blood. Nevertheless I say now, we'd better at least
listen to them."

"What?" T'heonax made round eyes. "I *hope* you
are joking."

Van Rijn rolled forth. "I got no time for fumblydid-
dles," he boomed. "You hear me, and I put it in
millicredit words so some two-year-old cub can explain
it to you. Look out there!" His arm waved broadly at
the sea. "We have rafts. Not so many, perhaps, but
enough. You make terms with us, or we keep on fighting. Soon it is you who do not have enough rafts. So!
Put that in your pipe and stick it!"

Wace nodded. Good. Good, indeed. Why had that
Drak'ho vessel run from his own lubber-manned prize?
It was willing enough to exchange long-range shots, or
to grapple sailor against sailor in the air. It was not
willing to risk being boarded, wrecked, or set ablaze by
Lannach's desperate devils.

Because it was a home, a fortress, and a
livelihood—the only way to make a living that this
culture knew. If you destroyed enough rafts, there
would not be enough fish-catching or fish-storing
capacity to keep the folk alive. It was as simple as that.

"We'll sink you!" screamed T'heonax. He stood
up, beating his wings, crest aquiver, tail held like an
iron bar. "We'll drown every last whelp of you!"

"Possible so," said Van Rijn. "This is supposed to
scare us? If we give up now, we are done for anyhow.
So we take you along to hell with us, to shine our shoes
and fetch us cool drinks, *nie?*"

Delp said, with trouble in his gaze: "We did not
come to Achan for love of destruction, but because
hunger drove us. It was you who denied us the right to
take fish which you yourselves never caught. Oh, yes,
we did take some of your land too, but the water we
must have. We can *not* give that up."

Van Rijn shrugged. "There are other seas. Maybe we let you haul a few more nets of fish before you go."

A captain of the Fleet said slowly: "My lord Delp has voiced the crux of the matter. It hints at a solution. After all, the Sea of Achan has little or no value to you Lannach'honai. We did, of course, wish to garrison your coasts, and occupy certain islands which are sources of timber and flint and the like. And naturally, we wanted a port of our own in Sagna Bay, for emergencies and repairs. These are questions of defense and self-suffiency, not of immediate survival like the water. So perhaps—"

"No!" cried T'heonax.

It was almost a scream. It shocked them into silence. The admiral crouched panting for a moment, then snarled at Tolk: "Tell your leader . . . I, the final authority . . . I refuse. I say we can crush your joke of a navy with small loss to ourselves. We have no reason to yield anything to you. We may allow you to keep the uplands of Lannach. That is the greatest concession you can hope for."

"Impossible!" spat the Herald. Then he rattled the translation off for Trolwen, who arched his back and bit the air.

"The mountains will not support us," explained Tolk more calmly. "We have already eaten them bare—that's no secret. We must have the lowlands. And we are certainly not going to let you hold any land whatsoever, to base an attack on us in a later year."

"If you think you can wipe us off the sea now, without a loss that will cripple you also, you may try," added Wace.

"I say we can!" stormed T'heonax. "And will!"

"My lord—" Delp hesitated. His eyes closed for a second. Then he said quite dispassionately: "My lord admiral, a finish fight now would likely be the end of our nation. Such few rafts as survived would be the prey of the first barbarian islanders that chanced along."

"And a retreat into The Ocean would *certainly* doom us," said T'heonax. His forefinger stabbed. "Unless you can conjure the trech and the fruitweed out of Achan and into the broad waters."

"That is true, of course, my lord," said Delp.

He turned and sought Trolwen's eyes. They regarded each other steadily, with respect.

"Herald," said Delp, "tell your chief this. We are not going to leave the Sea of Achan. We cannot. If you insist that we do so, we'll fight you and hope you can be destroyed without too much loss to ourselves. We have no choice in that matter.

"But I think maybe we can give up any thought of occupying either Lannach or Holmenach. You can keep all the solid land. We can barter our fish, salt, sea harvest, handicrafts, for your meat, stone, wood, cloth, and oil. It would in time become profitable for both of us."

"And incidental," said Van Rijn, "you might think of this bit too. If Drak'ho has no land, and Lannach has no ships, it will be sort of a little hard for one to make war on another, *nie?* After a few years, trading and getting rich off each other, you get so mutual dependent war is just impossible. So if you agree like now, soon your troubles are over, and then comes Nicholas van Rijn with Earth trade goods for all, like Father Christmas my prices are so reasonable. What?''

''Be still!'' shrieked T'heonax.

He grabbed the chief of his guards by a wing and pointed at Delp. ''Arrest that traitor!''

''My lord—'' Delp backed away. The guard hesitated. Delp's warriors closed in about their captain, menacingly. From the listening lower decks there came a groan.

''The Lodestar hear me,'' stammered Delp, ''I only suggested . . . I know the admiral has the final say—''

''And my say is, 'No.' '' declared T'heonax, tacitly dropping the matter of arrest. ''As admiral and Oracle, I forbid it. There is no possible agreement between the Fleet and these . . . these vile . . . filthy, dirty, animal—'' He dribbled at the lips. His hands curved into claws, poised above his head.

A rustle and murmur went through the ranked Drak'honai. The captains lay like winged leopards, still cloaked with dignity, but there was terror in their eyes. The Lannachska, ignorant of words but sensitive to tones, crowded together and gripped their weapons more tightly.

Tolk translated fast, in a low voice. When he had finished, Trolwen sighed.

''I hate to admit it,'' he said, ''but if you turn that *marswa's* words around, they are true. Do you really, seriously think two races as different as ours could live side by side? It would be too tempting to break the pledges. They could ravage our land while we were gone on migration, take all our towns again ... or we could come north once more with barbarian allies, bought with the promise of Drak'ho plunder— We'd be back at each other's throats, one way or another, in five years. Best to have it out now. Let the gods decide who's right and who's too depraved to live.''

Almost wearily, he bunched his muscles, to go down fighting if T'heonax ended the armistice this moment.

Van Rijn lifted his hands and his voice. It went like a bass drum, the length and breath and depth of the castle raft. And nocked arrows were slowly put back into their quivers.

"Hold still! Wait just a bloody minute, by damn. I am not through talking yet.''

He nodded curtly at Delp. "You have some sense, you. Maybe we can find a few others with brains not so much like a spoonful of moldy tea sold by my competitors. I am going to say something now. I will use Drak'ho language. Tolk, you make a running translation. This no one on the planet has heard before. I tell you Drak'ho and Lannacha are *not* alien! They are the same identical stupid race!''

Wace sucked in his breath. "What?'' he whispered in Anglic. "But the breeding cycles—''

"Kill me that fat worm!'' shouted T'heonax.

Van Rijn waved an impatient hand at him. "Be quiet, you. I make the talkings. So! Sit down, both you nations, and listen to Nicholas van Rijn!''

XX

The evolution of intelligent life on Diomedes is still largely conjectural; there has been no time to hunt fossils. But on the basis of existing biology and general principles, it is possible to reason out the course of millennial events.

Once upon a time in the planet's tropics there was a small continent or large island, thickly forested. The equatorial regions never know the long days and nights of high latitudes: at equinox the sun is up for six hours, to cross the sky and set for another six; at solstice there is a twilight, the sun just above or below the horizon. By Diomedean standards these are ideal conditions which will support abundant life. Among the species at this past epoch there was a small, bright-eyed arboreal carnivore. Like Earth's flying squirrel, it had developed a membrane on which to glide from branch to branch.

But a low-density planet has a queasy structure. Continents rise and sink with indecent speed, a mere few hundreds of thousands of years. Ocean and air currents are correspondingly deflected; and because of the great axial tilt and the larger fluid masses involved, Diomedean currents bear considerably more heat or cold than do Earth's. Thus, even at the equator, there were radical climatic shifts.

A period of drought shriveled the ancient forests into scattered woods separated by great dry pampas. The flying pseudo-squirrel developed true wings to go from copse to copse. But being an adaptable beast, it began also to prey on the new grass-eating animals which herded over the plains. To cope with the big ungulates, it grew in size. But then, needing more food to fuel the larger body, it was forced into a variety of environments, seashore, mountains, swamps—yet by virtue of mobility remained interbred rather than splitting into new species. A single individual might thus face many types of country in one lifetime, which put a premium on intelligence.

At this stage, for some unknown reason, the species—or a part of it, the part destined to become important—was forced out of the homeland. Possibly diastrophism broke the original continent into small islands which would not support so large an animal population; or the drying-out may have progressed still further. Whatever the cause, families and flocks drifted slowly northward and southward through hundreds of generations.

There they found new territories, excellent hunting—but a winter which they could not survive. When the long darkness came, they must perforce return to the tropics to wait for spring. It was not the inborn, automatic reaction of Terrestrial migratory birds. This animal was already too clever to be an instinct machine; its habits were *learned*. The brutal natural selection of the annual flights stimulated this intelligence yet more.

Now the price of intelligence is a very long childhood in proportion to the total lifespan. Since there is no action-pattern built into the thinker's genes, each generation must learn everything afresh, which takes time. Therefore no species can become intelligent unless it or its environment first produces some mechanism for keeping the parents together, so that they may protect the young during the extended period of helpless infancy and ignorant childhood. Mother love is not enough; Mother will have enough to do, tending the suicidally inquisitive cubs, without having to do all the food-hunting and guarding as well. Father must help out. But what will keep Father around, once his sexual urge has been satisfied?

Instinct can do it. Some birds, for example, employ both parents to rear the young. But elaborate instinctive compulsions are incompatible with intelligence. Father has to have a good selfish reason to stay, if Father has brains enough to *be* selfish.

In the case of man, the mechanism is simple: permanent sexuality. The human is never satisfied at any time of year. From this fact we derive the family, and hence the possibility of prolonged immaturity, and hence our cerebral cortex.

In the case of the Diomedean, there was migration. Each flock had a long and dangerous way to travel every year. It was best to go in company, under some form of organization. At journey's end in the tropics, there was the abandon of the mating season—but soon the unavoidable trip back home, for the equatorial islands would not support many visitors for very long.

Out of this primitive annual grouping—since it was not blindly instinctive, but the fruit of experience in a gifted animal—there grew loose permanent associations. Defensive bands became co-operative bands. Already the exigencies of travel had caused male and female to specialize their body types, one for fighting, one for burden-bearing. It was, therefore, advantageous that the sexes maintain their partnership the whole year around.

The animal of permanent family—on Diomedes, as a rule, a rather large family, an entire matrilineal clan—with the long gestation, the long cubhood, the constant change and challenge of environment, the competition for mates each midwinter with alien bands having alien ways: this animal had every evolutionary reason to start thinking. Out of such a matrix grew language, tools, fire, organized nations, and those vague unattainable yearnings we call "culture."

Now while the Diomedean had no irrevocable pattern of inborn behavior, he did tend everywhere to follow certain modes of life. They were the easiest. Analogously, humankind is not required by instinct to formalize and regulate its matings as marriage, but human societies have almost invariably done so. It is more comfortable for all concerned. And so the Diomedean migrated south to breed.

But he did not have to!

When breeding cycles exist, they are controlled by some simple foolproof mechanism. Thus, for many birds on Earth it is the increasing length of the day in springtime which causes mating: the optical stimulus triggers hormonal processes which reactivate the dormant gonads. On Diomedes, this wouldn't work; the light cycle varies too much with latitude. But once the proto-intelligent Diomedean had gotten into migratory habits—and therefore must breed only at a certain time of the year, if the young were to survive—evolution took the obvious course of making that migration itself the governor.

Ordinarily a hunter, with occasional meals of nuts or fruit or wild grain, the Diomedean exercised in spurts. Migration called for prolonged effort; it must have taken hundreds or thousands of generations to develop the flying muscles alone, time enough to develop other adaptations as well. So this effort stimulated certain glands, which operated through a complex hormonal system to waken the gonads. (An exception was the lactating female, whose mammaries secreted an inhibiting agent.) During the great flight, the sex hormone concentration built up—there was no time or energy to spare for its dissipation. Once in the tropics, rested and fed, the Diomedean made up for lost opportunities. He made up so thoroughly that the return trip had no significant effect on his exhausted glands.

Now and then in the homeland, fleetingly, after some unusual exertion, one might feel stirrings toward the opposite sex. One suppressed that, as rigorously as the human suppresses impulses to incest, and for an even more practical reason: a cub born out of season meant death on migration for itself as well as its mother. Not that the average Diomedean realized this overtly; he just accepted the taboo, founded religions and ethical systems and neuroses on it— However, doubtless the vague, lingering year-round attractiveness of the other sex had been an unconscious reason for the initial development of septs and flocks.

When the migratory Diomedean encountered a tribe which did not observe his most basic moral law, he knew physical horror.

Drak'ho Fleet was one of several which have now been discovered by traders. They may all have originated as groups living near the equator and thus not burdened by the need to travel; but this is still guesswork. The clear fact is that they began to live more off the sea than the land. Through many centuries they elaborated the physical apparatus of ships and tackle, until it had become their entire livelihood.

It gave more security than hunting. It gave a home which could be dwelt in continuously. It gave the possibility of constructing and using elaborate devices, accumulating large libraries, sitting and thinking or debating a problem—in short, the freedom to encumber oneself with a true civilization, which no migrator had except to the most limited degree. On the bad side, it meant grindingly hard labor and aristocratic domination.

This work kept the deckhand sexually stimulated; but warm shelters and stored sea food had made his birthtime independent of the season. Thus the sailor nations grew into a very humanlike pattern of marriage and child-raising: there was even a concept of romantic love.

The migrators, who thought him depraved, the sailor considered swinish. Indeed, neither culture could imagine how the other might even be of the same species.

And how shall one trust the absolute alien?

XXI

"It is these ideological pfuities that make the real nasty wars," said Van Rijn. "But now I have taken off the ideology and we can sensible and friendly settle down to swindling each other, *nie?*"

He had not, of course, explained his hypothesis in such detail. Lannach's philosophers had some vague idea of evolution, but were weak on astronomy; Drak'ho science was almost the reverse. Van Rijn had contented himself with very simple, repetitious words, sketching what must be the only reasonable explanation of the well-known reproductive differences.

He rubbed his hands and chortled into a tautening silence. "So! I have not made it all sweetness. Even I cannot do that overnights. For long times to come yet, you each think the others go about this in disgusting style. You make filthy jokes about each other . . . I know some good ones you can adapt. But you know, at least, that you are of the same race. Any of you could have been a solid member of the other nation, *nie?* Maybe, come changing times, you start switching around your ways to live. Why not experiment a little, ha? No, no, I see you can not like that idea yet, I say no more."

He folded his arms and waited, bulky, shaggy, ragged, and caked with the grime of weeks. On creaking planks, under a red sun and a low sea wind, the scores of winged warriors and captains shuddered in the face of the unimagined.

Delp said at last, so slow and heavy it did not really break that drumhead silence: "Yes. This makes sense. I believe it."

After another minute, bowing his head toward stone-rigid T'heonax: "My lord, this does change the situation. I think—it will not be as much as we hoped for, but better than I feared—We can make terms, they to have all the land and we to have the Sea of Achan. Now that I know they are not . . . devils . . . animals —Well, the normal guarantees, oaths and exchange of hostages and so on—should make the treaty firm enough."

Tolk had been whispering in Trolwen's ear. Lannach's commander nodded. "That is much my own thought," he said.

"Can we persuade the Council and the clans, Flockchief?" muttered Tolk.

"Herald, if we bring back an honorable peace, the Council will vote our ghosts godhood after we die."

Tolk's gaze shifted back to T'heonax, lying without movement among his courtiers. And the grizzled fur lifted along the Herald's back.

"Let us first return to the Council alive, Flock-chief," he said.

T'heonax rose. His wings beat the air, cracking noises like an ax going through bone. His muzzle wrinkled into a lion mask, long teeth gleamed wetly forth, and he roared:

"No! I've heard enough! This farce is at an end!"

Trolwen and the Lannacha escort did not need an interpreter. They clapped hands to weapons and fell into a defensive circle. Their jaws clashed shut automatically, biting the wind.

"My lord!" Delp sprang fully erect.

"Be still!" screeched T'heonax. "You've said far too much." His head swung from side to side. "Captains of the Fleet, you have heard how Delp hyr Orikan advocates making peace with creatures lower than the beasts. Remember it!"

"But my lord—" An older officer stood up, hands aloft in protest. "My lord admiral, we've just had it shown to us, they aren't beasts . . . it's only a different—"

"Assuming the Eart'ho spoke truth, which is by no means sure, what of it?" T'heonax fleered at Van Rijn. "It only makes the matter worse. We know beasts can't help themselves but these Lannach'honai are dirty by choice. And you would let them live? You would . . . would *trade* with them . . . enter their towns . . . let your young be seduced into their —No!"

The captains looked at each other. It was like an audible groan. Only Delp seemed to have the courage to speak again.

"I humbly beg the admiral to recall, we've no real choice. If we fight them to a finish, it may be our own finish too."

"Ridiculous!" snorted T'heonax. "Either you are afraid or they've bribed you."

Tolk had been translating *sotto voce* for Trolwen. Now, sickly, Wace heard the commander's grim reply to his Herald: "If he takes that attitude, a treaty is out of the question. Even if he made it, he'd sacrifice his hostages to us—not to speak of ours to him—just to renew the war whenever he felt ready. Let's get back before I myself violate the truce!"

And there, thought Wace, *is the end of the world. I will die under flung stones, and Sandra will die in Glacier Land. Well . . . we tried.*

He braced himself. The admiral might not let this embassy depart.

Delp was looking around from face to face. "Captains of the Fleet," he cried, "I ask your opinion . . . I implore you, persuade my lord admiral that—"

"The next treasonable word uttered by anyone will cost him his wings," shouted T'heonax. "Or do you question my authority?"

It was a bold move, thought Wace in a distant part of his thuttering brain—to stake all he had on that one challenge. But of course, T'heonax was going to get away with it; no one in this caste-ridden society would deny his absolute power, not even Delp the bold. Reluctant they might be, but the captains would obey.

The silence grew shattering.

Nicholas van Rijn broke it with a long, juicy Bronx cheer.

The whole assembly started. T'heonax leaped backward and for a moment he was like a bat-winged tomcat.

"What was that?" he blazed.

"Are you deaf?" answered Van Rijn mildly. "I said—" He repeated with tremolo.

"What do you mean?"

"It is an Earth term," said Van Rijn. "As near as I can render it, let me see . . . well, it means you are a—" The rest was the most imaginative obscenity Wace had heard in his life.

The captains gasped. Some drew their weapons. The Drak'ho guards on the upper decks gripped bows and spears. "Kill him!" screamed T'heonax.

"No!" Van Rijn's bass exploded on their ears. The sheer volume of it paralyzed them. "I am an embassy, by damn! You hurt an embassy and the Lodestar will sink you in hell's boiling seas!"

It checked them. T'heonax did not repeat his order; the guards jerked back toward stillness; the officers remained poised, outraged past words.

"I have somethings to say you," Van Rijn continued, only twice as loud as a large foghorn. "I speak to all the Fleet, and ask you ask yourselves, why this little pip squeaker does so stupid. He makes you carry on a war where both sides lose—he makes you risk your lives, your wives and cubs, maybe the Fleet's own surviving—why? Because he is afraid. He knows, a

few years cheek by jowl next to the Lannach'honai, and
even more so trading with my company at my fantastic
low prices, things begin to change. You get more into
thinking by your own selves. You taste freedom. Bit by
bit, his power slides from him. And he is too much a
coward to live on his own selfs. *Nie,* he has got to have
guards and slaves and all of you to make bossing over,
so he proves to himself he is not just a little jellypot but
a real true Leader. Rather he will have the Fleet ruined,
even die himself, than lose this propup, him!''

T'heonax said, shaking: "Get off my raft before I
forget there is an armistice.''

"Oh, I go, I go,'' said Van Rijn. He advanced toward the admiral. His tread reverberated in the deck. "I
go back and make war again if you insist. But only one
small question I ask first.'' He stopped before the royal
presence and prodded the royal nose with a hairy
forefinger. "Why you make so much fuss about Lannacha home lifes? Could be maybe down underneath
you hanker to try it yourself?''

He turned his back, then, and bowed.

Wace did not see just what happened. There were
guards and captains between. He heard a screech, a
bellow from Van Rijn, and then there was a hurricane
of wings before him.

Something— He threw himself into the press of
bodies. A tail crashed against his ribs. He hardly felt it;
his fist jolted, merely to get a warrior out of the way and
see—

Nicholas van Rijn stood with both hands in the air as
a score of spears menaced him. "The admiral bit me!''

he wailed. ''I am here like an embassy, and the pig bites me! What kind of relations between countries is that, when heads of state bite foreign ambassadors, ha? Does an Earth president bite diplomats? This is uncivilized!''

T'heonax backed off, spitting, scrubbing the blood from his jaws. ''Get out,'' he said in a strangled voice. ''Go at once.''

Van Rijn nodded. ''Come, friends,'' he said. ''We find us places with better manners.''

''Freeman . . . Freeman, where did he—'' Wace crowded close.

''Never mind where,'' said Van Rijn huffily.

Trolwen and Tolk joined them. The Lannacha escort fell into step behind. They walked at a measured pace across the deck, away from the confusion of Drak'honai under the castle wall.

''You might have known it,'' said Wace. He felt exhausted, drained of everything except a weak anger at his chief's unbelievable folly. ''This race is carnivorous. Haven't you seen them snap when they get angry? It's . . . a reflex— You might have known!''

''Well,'' said Van Rijn in a most virtuous tone, holding both hands to his injury, ''he did not *have* to bite. I am not responsible for his lack of control or any consequences of it, me. All good lawyer saints witness I am not.''

''But the ruckus—we could all have been killed!''

Van Rijn didn't bother to argue about that.

Delp met them at the rail. His crest drooped. ''I am sorry it must end thus,'' he said. ''We could have been friends.''

"Perhaps it does not end just so soon," said Van Rijn.

"What do you mean?" Tired eyes regarded him without hope.

"Maybe you see pretty quick. Delp"—Van Rijn laid a paternal hand on the Drak'ho's shoulder—"you are a good young chap. I could use a one like you, as a part-time agent for some tradings in these parts. On fat commissions, natural. But for now, remember you are the one they all like and respect. If anything happens to the admiral, there will be panic and uncertainty . . . they will turn to you for advice. If you act fast at such a moment, you can be admiral yourself! Then maybe we do business, ha?"

He left Delp gaping and swung himself with apish speed down into the canoe. "Now, boys," he said, "row like hell."

They were almost back to their own fleet when Wace saw clotted wings whirl up from the royal raft. He gulped. "Has the attack . . . has it begun already?" He cursed himself that his voice should be an idiotic squeak.

"Well, I am glad we are not close to them." Van Rijn, standing up as he had done the whole trip, nodded complacently. "But I think not this is the war. I think they are just disturbed. Soon Delp will take charge and calms them down."

"But—*Delp?*"

Van Rijn shrugged. "If Diomedean proteins is deadly to us," he said, "ours should not be so good for them, ha? And our late friend T'heonax took a big mouthful of me. It all goes to show, these foul tempers only lead to trouble. Best you follow my example. When I am attacked, I turn the other cheek.''

XXII

Thursday Landing had little in the way of hospital facilities: an autodiagnostician, a few surgical and therapeutical robots, the standard drugs, and the post xenobiologist to double as medical officer. But a six weeks' fast did not have serious consequences, if you were strong to begin with and had been waited on hand, foot, wing, and tail by two anxious nations, on a planet none of whose diseases could affect you. Treatment progressed rapidly with the help of bioaccelerine, from intravenous glucose to thick rare steaks. By the sixth Diomedean day, Wace had put on a noticeable amount of flesh and was weakly but fumingly aprowl in his room.

"Smoke, sir?" asked young Benegal. He had been out on trading circuit when the rescue party arrived;

only now was he getting the full account. He offered cigarettes with a most respectful air.

Wace halted, the bathrobe swirling about his knees. He reached, hesitated, then grinned and said: "In all that time without tobacco, I seem to've lost the addiction. Question is, should I go to the trouble and expense of building it up again?"

"Well, no, sir—"

"Hey! Gimme that!" Wace sat down on his bed and took a cautious puff. "I certainly am going to pick up all my vices where I left off, and doubtless add some new ones."

"You, uh, you were going to tell me, sir . . . how the station here was informed—"

"Oh, yes. That. It was childishly simple. I figured it out in ten minutes, once we got a breathing spell. Send a fair-size Diomedean party with a written message, plus of course one of Tolk's professional interpreters to help them inquire their way on this side of The Ocean. Devise a big life raft, just a framework of light poles which could be dovetailed together. Each Diomedean carried a single piece; they assembled it in the air and rested on it whenever necessary. Also fished from it: a number of Fleet experts went along to take charge of that angle. There was enough rain for them to catch in small buckets to drink—I knew there would be, since the Drak'honai stay at sea for indefinite periods, and also this is such a rainy planet anyhow.

"Incidentally, for reasons which are now obvious to you, the party had to include some Lannacha females. Which means that the messengers of both nationalities have had to give up some hoary prejudices. In the long run, that's going to change their history more than whatever impression we Terrestrials might have made, by such stunts as flying them home across The Ocean in a single day. From now on, willy-nilly, the beings who went on that trip will be a subversive element in both cultures; they'll be the seedbed of Diomedean internationalism. But that's for the League to gloat about, not me.''

Wace shrugged. ''Having seen them off,'' he finished, ''we could only crawl into bed and wait. After the first few days, it wasn't so bad. Appetite disappears.''

He stubbed out the cigarette with a grimace. It was making him dizzy.

''When do I get to see the others?''he demanded. ''I'm strong enough now to feel bored. I want company, dammit.''

''As a matter of fact, sir,'' said Benegal, ''I believe Freeman van Rijn said something about''—a thunderous *''Skulls and smallpox!''* bounced in the corridor outside—''visiting you today.''

''Run along then,'' said Wace sardonically. ''You're too young to hear this. We blood brothers, who have defied death together, we sworn comrades, and so on and so forth, are about to have a reunion.''

He got to his feet as the boy slipped out the back door. Van Rijn rolled in the front entrance.

His Jovian girth was shrunken flat, he had only one chin, and he leaned on a gold-headed cane. But his hair was curled into oily black ringlets, his mustaches and goatee waxed to needle points, his lace-trimmed shirt and cloth-of-gold vest were already smeared with snuff, his legs were hairy tree trunks beneath a batik sarong, he wore a diamond mine on each hand and a silver chain about his neck which could have anchored a battleship. He waved a ripe Trichinopoly cigar above a four-decker sandwich and roared:

"So you are walking again. Good fellow! The only way you get well is not sip dishwater soup and take it easily, like that upgebungled horse doctor has the nerve to tell me to do." He purpled with indignation. "Does one thought get through that sand in his synapses, what it is costing me every hour I wait here? What a killing I can make if I get home among those underhand competition jackals before the news reaches them Nicholas van Rijn is alive after all? I have just been out beating the station engineer over his thick flat mushroom he uses for a head, telling him if my spaceship is not ready to leave tomorrow noon I will hitch him to it and say giddap. So you will come back to Earth with us your own selfs, *nie?*"

Wace had no immediate reply. Sandra had followed the merchant in.

She was driving a wheelchair, and looked so white and thin that his heart cracked over. Her hair was a pale frosty cloud on the pillow, it seemed as if it would be cold to touch. But her eyes lived, immense, the infinite warm green of Earth's gentlest seas; and she smiled at him.

"My lady—" he whispered.

"Oh, she comes too," said Van Rijn, selecting an

apple from the fruit basket at Wace's bedside. "We all continue our interrupted trip, maybe with not so much fun and games aboard—" He drooped one little sleet-gray eye at her, lasciviously. "Those we save for later on Earth when we are back to normal, ha?"

"If my lady has the strength to travel—" stumbled Wace. He sat down, his knees would bear him no longer.

"Oh, yes," she murmured. "It is only a matter of following the diet as written for me and getting much rest."

"Worst thing you can do, by damn," grumbled Van Rijn, finishing the apple and picking up an orange.

"It isn't suitable," protested Wace. "We lost so many servants when the skycruiser ditched. She'd only have—"

"A single maid to attend me?" Sandra's laugh was ghostly, but it held genuine amusement. "After now I am to forget what we did and endured, and be so correct and formal with you, Eric? That would be most silly, when we have climbed the ridge over Salmenbrok together, not?"

Wace's pulse clamored. Van Rijn, strewing orange peel on the floor, said: "Out of hard lucks, the good Lord can pull much money if He chooses. I cannot know every man in the company, so promising youngsters like you do go sometimes to waste on little outposts like here. Now I will take you home to Earth and find a proper paying job for you."

If *she* could remember one chilled morning beneath Mount Oborch, thought Wace, he, for the sake of his manhood, could remember less pleasant things, and name them in plain words. It was time.

He was still too weak to rise—he shook a little—but he caught Van Rijn's gaze and said in a voice hard with anger:

"That's the easiest way to get back your self-esteem, of course. Buy it! Bribe me with a sinecure to forget how Sandra sat with a paintbrush in a coalsack of a room, till she fainted from exhaustion, and how she gave us her last food . . . how I myself worked my brain and my heart out to pull us all back from that jailhouse country and win a war to boot—No, don't interrupt. I know you had some part in it. You fought during that naval engagement: because you had no choice, no place to hide. You found a nice nasty way to dispose of an inconvenient obstacle to the peace negotiations. You have a talent for that sort of thing. And you made some suggestions.

"But what did it amount to? It amount to your saying to me: 'Do this! Build that!' And I had to do it, with nonhuman helpers and stoneage tools. I had to design it, even! Any fool could once have said, 'Take me to the Moon.' It took brains to figure out how!

"Your role, your 'leadership,' amounted to strolling around, gambling and chattering, playing cheap politics, eating like a hippopotamus while Sandra lay starving on Dawrnach—and claiming all the credit! And now I'm supposed to go to Earth, sit down in a gilded pigpen of an office, spend the rest of my life thumb-twiddling . . . and keep quiet when you brag. Isn't that right? You and your sinecure—"

Wace saw Sandra's eyes on him, grave, oddly compassionate, and jerked to a halt.

"I quit," he ended.

Van Rijn had swallowed the orange and returned to his sandwich during Wace's speech. Now he burped, licked his fingers, took a fresh puff of his cigar, and rumbled quite mildly:

"If you think I give away sinecures, you are being too optimist. I am offering you a job with importance for no reason except I think you can do it better than some knucklebone heads on Earth. I will pay you what the job is worth. And by damn, you will work your promontory off."

Wace gulped after air.

"Go ahead and insult me, public if you wish," said Van Rijn. "Just not on company time. Now I go find me who it was put the bomb in that cruiser and take care of him. Also maybe the cook will fix me a little Italian hero sandwich. Death and dynamite, they want to starve me to bones here, them!"

He waved a shaggy paw and departed like an amiable earthquake.

Sandra wheeled over and laid on a hand on Wace's. It was a cool touch, light as a leaf falling in a northern October, but it burned him. As if from far off, he heard her:

"I awaited this to come, Eric. It is best you understand now. I, who was born to govern . . . my whole life has been a long governing, not? . . . I know what I speak of. There are the fake leaders, the balloons, with talent only to get in people's way. Yes. But he is

not one of them. Without him, you and I would sleep
dead beneath Achan.''

"But—"

"You complain he made you do the hard things that
used your talent, not his? Of course he did. It is not the
leader's job to do everything himself. It is his job to
order, persuade, wheedle, bully, bribe—just that, to
make people do what must be done, whether or not they
think it is possible.

"You say, he spent time loafing around talking,
making jokes and a false front to impress the natives?
Of course! Somebody had to. We were monsters,
strangers, beggars as well. Could you or I have started
as a deformed beggar and ended as all but king?

"You say he bribed—with goods from crooked
dice—and blustered, lied, cheated, politicked, killed
both open and sly? Yes. I do not say it was right. I do
not say he did not enjoy himself, either. But can you
name another way to have gotten our lives back? Or
even to make peace for those poor warring devils?''

"Well . . . well—" The man looked away, out the
window to the stark landscape. It would be good to
dwell inside Earth's narrower horizon.

"Well, maybe," he said at last, grudging each word.
"I . . . I suppose I was too hasty. Still—we played our
parts too, you know. Without us, he—"

"I think, without us, he would have found some
other way to come home," she interrupted. "But we
without him, no."

He jerked his head back. Her face was burning a
deeper red than the ember sunlight outside could tinge
it.

He thought, with sudden weariness: *After all, she is a woman, and women live more for the next generation than men can. Most especially she does, for the life of a planet may rest on her child, and she is an aristocrat in the old pure meaning of the word. He who fathers the next Duke of Hermes may be aging, fat, and uncouth; callous and conscienceless; unable to see her as anything but a boisterous episode. It doesn't matter, if the woman and the aristocrat see him as a man.*

Well-a-day, I have much to thank them both for.

"I—" Sandra looked confused, almost trapped. Her look held an inarticulate pleading. "I think I had best go and let you rest." After a moment of his silence: "He is not yet so strong as he claims. I may be needed."

"No," said Wace with an enormous tenderness. "The need is all yours. Good-by, my lady."

POUL ANDERSON

Ursula K. Le Guin

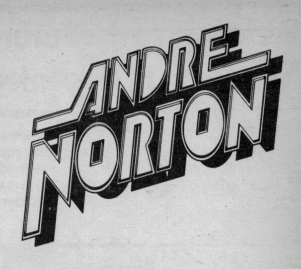

89705	**Witch World**	$1.95
87875	**Web of the Witch World**	$1.95
80805	**Three Against the Witch World**	$1.95
87323	**Warlock of the Witch World**	$1.95
77555	**Sorceress of the Witch World**	$1.95
94254	**Year of the Unicorn**	$1.95
82356	**Trey of Swords**	$1.95
95490	**Zarsthor's Bane** (Illustrated)	$1.95